FATAL DESIRES

Fatal Cross Live!

Book 1

Disclaimer:

This book is a work of fiction. Any resemblance to any person, living or dead is purely coincidental. The names of people, places, and/or things are all created from the author's mind and are only used for entertainment.

Due to the content, this book is recommended for adults **18 years and/or older**.

Please be aware, this book contains scenes relating to and the discussion of illegal drugs.

ISBN: 978-1515148166

Cover Design:
Custom eBook Covers

Cover Photographer:
Eric David Battershell

Cover Model:
Derrick Meacham

Editing by:
Heidi Ryan

Formatted by:
Wayne Hissong

Published by:
Theresa Hissong

For more information or how to contact
Theresa Hissong:

http://authortheresahissong.com
www.facebook.com/authortheresahissong

Other Books by Theresa Hissong:

A Glory Days Production:
Sing to Me
Save Me
Deliver Me

A Glory Days Awakening:
Wait for Me
Take Me
Accept Me

A Glory Days Reunion:
Understand Me
Beg Me
Break Me

A Glory Days Finale:
Need Me
Burn Me
Finish Me

Warriors of the Krieger:
Blood & Roses
Blood at Stake

Book for Charity:
Fully Loaded

Dedication:

To new friends and old…

I'm a firm believer that things happen for a

reason. I'm also a firm believer that a person is

put into your path for a reason.

To those of you who have crossed my path

and brightened my day, encouraging me to

reach for my dreams…thank you!

This one is for you.

Contents

PROLOGUE

Coraline

One night of heated passion with Taylor Vaughn and three store-bought pregnancy tests later, I was fucked. Totally screwed.

I was freaking pregnant!

And that low-down, dirty piece of shit wouldn't return my calls.

Taylor showing up at the same resort as me was just a coincidence...my ass. We'd both been flirtatious on the tour a year ago when his band, *Fatal Cross*, opened for *Glory Days*, my cousin's band. I'd been a roadie and tour manager for *Glory Days* for the past six years. Ever since the day I graduated high school, I had worked my ass off to make their concerts the best of the best. That's how the current events leading up to this point in my life happened. I ended up lusting over the guitarist for *Fatal Cross* when they'd opened for *Glory Days* just one year ago.

It wasn't until three weeks ago that I saw Taylor in the Azores at a resort I *thought* was private.

A shadow had formed over my lawn chair and I raised my sunglasses to see who the hell was bothering me. I was completely surprised to see the sexy guitarist hovering over my chair like a dog in heat. Of course, his eyes heated from roaming up and down the navy blue string bikini I was wearing. And you better believe I flaunted my goods for him to see. We were on neutral turf, and I didn't have to keep to my self-imposed rules of business only relationships with the people I dealt with on a day to day basis.

Dinner and two bottles of very expensive wine later, we were tearing each other's clothes off like pornstars just offered a million dollar contract.

It was a curse that sex with Taylor was the best sex I'd ever had. It was also a given that sex that good should've come with a warning label, because nothing said I'd get knocked up with his kid. Of course, at the time, I really didn't care when he was buried to the hilt and I was screaming his name.

My birth control obviously didn't work or I'd have made him use some sort of protection. That was the other dumbass move on my part. Rule number one....don't sleep with rockstars who've dipped their pen in so much ink that their cocks are stained from all the attention.

Now, I had to get in touch with him and he wasn't answering my calls or returning my messages. The whole thing was nothing but a one night stand, and the sad thing was…I wanted more. Even if he was the biggest jerk on the face of the planet, I still wanted him. We clicked in ways I'd never had with another man. He got me, but obviously the feelings were one-sided.

Standing in the bathroom of my condo in Los Angeles, and looking at the pregnancy tests lined up on the sink, I realized that I was a fool. Taylor Vaughn didn't want anything from me but a hot night in the sack. I was a conquest. He'd scaled that mountain and posted his flag at the peak.

And the kicker? In just two months' time, he will be taking over for *Glory Days* guitarist, Gabe Miller, while he returned home for the birth of his child. I'll be screwed, because with my line of work and being pregnant, I won't be doing much more than being the band's gofer, and Taylor will definitely know that I am pregnant as soon as I start showing. I didn't mind about the work situation, but I was sure that once my cousin found out about the little bun in my oven, Taylor Vaughn was a dead man.

CHAPTER 1

Coraline

Sleep still clogged my brain as I was jolted awake by a strange feeling in my gut. My stomach hurt, and I had no desire to get out of bed. It had to be super early in the morning or the middle of the night, because everything was dark outside my window.

I gasped when another cramp rolled deep in my stomach, and that's when I felt something hot and wet between my legs. I scrambled out of bed and ran to the bathroom, crying out in fear when I realized that I was bleeding…a lot.

"Oh, fuck," I gasped, grabbing a clean towel out of the linen closet by the door. Another cramp caused me to groan. I knew what was happening, but I was too panicked to shed tears. I had to get to the hospital, but there was no way I could drive in this condition.

I cleaned up as best as I could and grabbed a clean pair of panties and a pad. I climbed back up on my bed, avoiding the large spot of blood on the sheets. I picked up my phone and dialed the only person who would come for me this time of night.

"Cora, what's wrong?" Kane gasped, answering the phone. His voice was rough with sleep, but the concern was there in his deep baritone voice. My cousin was the only family I kept close. He was the one who practically raised me and protected me while I was growing up.

"Kane, I need you to take me to the hospital," I said, trying my best not to break down in tears. It was hard to admit to myself that I knew what was happening. I was losing the baby.

"What's wrong?" he demanded.

"Kane, just…just come to my place, please?" I begged, the tears breaking through and spilling down my cheeks. "I'll explain everything when you get here. Please…hurry."

"I'm coming," he said, already calling out for his bodyguard, Sergi, to stay with his wife, Delilah, and their daughters.

I squeezed my legs tightly together, hoping that would somehow help keep the baby inside me. I laid on my side and prayed that everything was going to be okay.

This whole situation was even more fucked up now. I was losing a baby I didn't even know if I wanted to keep. I was only twenty-four, for heaven's sake! I was too damn young to be a mom and had too much going on in my life to put my career on hold to raise a kid. The only thing I knew how to do was set up stage lights and run a schedule for four rockstars on a nightly basis. I couldn't, and wouldn't, put a kid through that type of life. So maybe this was a blessing in disguise?

It was fifteen minutes before Kane came bursting through my door with Delilah right behind him. "Cora!" I should've known that my best friend, who'd married my cousin, wouldn't have let Kane come alone.

"In here," I called out. I squeezed my eyes closed and wiped away tears when I heard them curse upon entering my room.

"Oh God, Cora," Delilah choked out, her eyes wide with fright at finding me lying next to blood soaked sheets. She hurried up on the bed and sat behind me, rubbing her hands over my chilled arms. "What happened?"

"Talk to me," Kane demanded, leaning over so that we were nose to nose. His hazel eyes flared with anger and worry. Kane was my cousin, my protector, and my best friend.

"I'm pregnant...and I think I'm having a miscarriage," I cried. If anyone would be understanding, it would be Kane and Delilah, but that didn't mean that Kane would be happy when he found out who the baby belonged to.

"D, lock up behind us," he ordered, scooping me up into his arms. I rested my head on his shoulder and wrapped my arms around his neck. His masculine scent felt like home and reminded me of when I was a little girl. Kane had always been there to patch up my scraped knees or to defend me when I couldn't defend myself. "I got you."

"I'm sorry," I said, squeezing him tighter. Kane was the closest thing I had to a brother, and I loved him more than he would ever know. My dad wasn't around much and my mom died when I was a very young, leaving me alone and without any supervision. Kane practically raised me, and ever since I can remember, we were inseparable.

"No need to be sorry, cuz," he said, laying me across the backseat of the SUV he'd driven to my house. I noticed his muscled jaw tick as he clamped his lips shut to keep from asking me any other questions. His hazel eyes were masked with worry as he nodded and turned to get into the driver's seat.

Delilah climbed in the back of the truck and pulled my head into her lap, "How long have you been bleeding?" She stroked my short black hair, brushing my bangs off my forehead.

"I don't know," I admitted, fresh tears rolling down my face. I was too tired and worried to wipe them away. "I woke up having cramps, and I'd been bleeding in my sleep. I called you right away." My eyes flickered to the front of the vehicle and met with Kane's in the rearview mirror. I caught a look of panic flash across my cousin's face. I immediately felt horrible for being the cause of his worry, but I'd never needed him like I needed him now.

Kane snapped his seatbelt in place and drove at breakneck speed to the hospital that was only fifteen minutes from my condo. He was quiet during the ride, and I knew it was killing him not to ask me how I could be so stupid as to get pregnant. I guess it didn't matter now that Taylor never returned my calls. *God, I was so fucking dumb!*

"Don't cry, Cora," Delilah whispered, stroking the hair back from my face again. It felt nice, in a motherly way. Something I hadn't had in many years.

Delilah had been my friend since before I'd graduated from high school. I'd worked at a local venue on weekends, learning the ropes to be the best roadie I could be. When she came through town, working for another band, we'd struck up a friendship that had lasted for several years.

Our roles had reversed, though. It'd been me, at one time, who was rushing her to get medical help for the injuries she'd sustained when her ex beat her almost to the point of death. Now, she held me as I cried for an unborn baby I didn't even have inside me for long enough to get comfortable with the fact that I'd been pregnant.

"Who do I need to call, Cora?" Delilah whispered, her eyes darting to the back of her husband's head. "Who is the father?"

"He doesn't know," I breathed, my voice barely above a whisper. "I don't want him to know."

"Who, Coraline?" Kane asked from the front seat. His voice was strained and tight as he glanced over his shoulder.

"Please, Kane, not now," I cried. Squeezing my eyes closed, I prayed we'd get to the hospital in time. Or was it too late already?

"Fuck, Coraline," he cursed, pushing the accelerator a little harder. I flinched when he slammed his hand down on the steering wheel. "God damn it, Cora. Who the fuck knocked you up?"

"*Kane,*" Delilah growled a warning. Her voice sent his attention back to the road.

We arrived at the hospital, and I was taken back immediately. Kane and Delilah stayed in the waiting room while I was looked over by a doctor.

The next few hours were the most emotionally painful of my entire life.

CHAPTER 2

Taylor

"Are you going to answer that?" Cash asked from beside me in the Tahoe we were riding in to the studio.

"Not yet," I lied. It was Cora. She'd called three times in the past two days, but I couldn't answer it. Not after the bullshit I'd pulled with her and not calling after we'd gotten lost in each other on that island. I should've called her the next morning, or the morning after that, but I just…didn't. Now it was a month later, and I'd probably screwed up any chance I had with getting her into my bed for round two.

My only saving grace was the upcoming tour with *Glory Days*. I knew she'd be there, and I hoped that I'd be able to sit her down and apologize in person. Over the phone just wasn't the way to make amends.

Something about that little pixie drew me in like a starving man about to eat his first meal. When I touched her for the first time, it felt like I was coming home, and that scared me senseless. Coraline Maddox was not the type of woman who'd wait for their man to come home after being out on the road. She was one of us and lived the way we lived whenever she was out on tour with her cousin's band. That girl had fire and a mouth on her that makes a man want to kiss her until she shut up or hog tie her to the bed until she submitted.

She's exactly what I wanted and needed in my life. Dating was always a hardship, though. Most people believed that it was all fun and games dating a rockstar, but they're wrong. It's hard ass work, with sleepless nights and hours upon hours of traveling. Not knowing when I'd be home to a girlfriend was hard on all parties involved.

Yeah…then there's Cora. She got the business we're in and she got me, more than I ever thought a woman could. That Maddox girl was getting under my skin and I didn't want to want her, but I did. And that just pissed me off, because I was not boyfriend material. My job kept me too busy to maintain a healthy relationship with a woman as deserving as Cora.

I'd been playing the part of a Casanova for the past few years, never keeping a woman to warm my sheets any longer than one night. Hell…usually, I'd show them the door before they wanted to cuddle and talk. All of them knew that before climbing into the sack with me, because I'd made myself perfectly clear. The only woman I did not say that to was Cora.

And the worst part of this? The fact that since Coraline and I had shared that night together a month ago, I hadn't even looked at another woman…hadn't even entertained the thought of sex when it'd been offered to me, because some portion of my brain would bring up images of the sexy, tough-as-nails roadie, and I couldn't even come up to bat, so to speak.

Whatever the hell was wrong with me, it needed to stop, and stop soon. I had an album to write and record, then hit the road in two months with *Glory Days* to fill in for their guitarist while he was home with his wife and new baby.

"We're here," Cash said, pulling me back from my internal ass kicking. Cash, our bassist, had driven from his home over on the Olympic Peninsula and picked us up at my place in the city.

We walked into the studio we were using in downtown Seattle to record a few demos for the upcoming album. We all groaned when the scent of weed hit us like a brick fucking wall. I covered my nose and cursed before turning around and propping the outside door open.

The band before us was doing more partying than recording.

"Hey, man," some red-eyed kid slurred, raising his hand for a high-five. We all nodded, but didn't touch him as we passed him in the hallway. Thankfully, he got the hint and didn't reply. I would not give this guy the satisfaction of any type of joy about meeting him and his buddies.

"Sorry," Mitch, the producer, frowned as we found him putting away some files at his desk.

"We don't care what you do, Mitch," Cash sighed. "But we need to air the place out. We don't need to be around that shit."

"Gotcha, man," Mitch said, jumping to his feet and heading toward the back door. He propped it open and the cross breeze pushed the cloud of smoke toward the front of the building. "So, I'm guessing you guys are still clean?"

"Yeah," I answered. It was well known that we'd had our fair share of parties since we'd started this band, and it was also well known that the band had all taken a year off to spend in drug rehab to stop the addictions that were slowly killing us.

"Good," he nodded. "That's good to hear. You guys ready to work?"

"Ready as we'll ever be," I declared, setting my guitar case down against the wall.

Braxton Keller, our new drummer, was the last in the door and he groaned when he caught the unmistakable scent in the air. "Really? Are you fucking serious?" he growled angrily. He'd had his own run-ins with drugs and we forged a bond between the four of us when we signed him on after losing our last drummer for attempting to rape the wife of our dear friend Reed Sullivan, who is also the baby sister of Gabe Miller from the band *Glory Days*.

"Five minutes and you'll never know what went on here," Mitch promised as he produced a can of air freshener and proceeded to use half of the can to cover up the smell. Of course, it didn't work.

It took twenty minutes before we were able to sit down with our songs and go over them with Mitch. The thing about Mitch was, he was the best damn producer on the West Coast and worth every penny spent to have his name on our album.

Braxton was tense and I couldn't blame the guy. He'd been clean for three years now, just a few months less than us. He'd turned his life around so much so, you wouldn't even recognize him. Gone was the tall, skinny drummer, and in his place was a giant. His fucking arms were the size of boulders and I wouldn't piss him off on his best day. The guy was quiet and that just made him scary as hell. His light brown hair was brushed back out of his face and his eyes were so fierce, he could pierce you with an angry stare from a block away.

It didn't take long before we started recording our first song on the new album. I played for hours that day and felt good about actually recording without being high. Ace sang as if his life depended on it, and I was smiling by the time we loaded up to head back to our homes.

That day would end up being one of the hardest days I'd faced in the past two years.

After I'd arrived home, a knock on my door had me cursing when I opened it, wanting to slam the door in the guy's face.

"Hey, T," Jared greeted, holding out his hand. Seeing the man who'd supplied my habit for six years was not what I needed at the moment.

"What do you want?" I avoided his touch and crossed my arms over my chest as I blocked the doorway, silently telling him he wasn't going to step foot over my threshold.

"I've got some stuff you like," he smirked. "I'll even cut you a deal on the K. What do you say?" K, meaning kilo.

"Fuck no," I growled. "Man, I'm clean and have no damn desire to start that shit back up again."

"Not even for an old friend?" he smiled, hoping to make a deal. Jared was a pretty boy, nothing like the drug dealers you see portrayed on television. No, this guy took his daddy's money and started an empire, selling drugs to the rich and famous. There were no back alley transactions done by him or any of his crew.

"You know damn good and well that we are not friends," I seethed, clenching my fists. I'd beat the hell out of this guy if he didn't leave…soon. I didn't need, or want, this shit in my life again. It'd almost killed me once. "Now, get the fuck out of here and don't come back. Got me?"

"Damn, dude," he frowned. "Thought I'd help a brother out."

"Well, you're not helping," I scoffed, placing my hand on the door, ready to close it in his face. I wasn't stupid. I knew this guy carried a gun, and from the bulge at his hip, I knew he was packing heat. *Fuck, I don't need this shit today!*

"Here," he insisted, tossing something at my chest. I automatically caught the small, clear baggie, dropping it like it was on fire as soon as I realized what it contained. "What? You don't want a taste? It's on me. Call me if you change your mind, but don't wait long."

"I *told* you," I roared, bending over to pick up the baggie filled with cocaine. "I don't want it or fucking need it. Take this shit and do not ever come back!" My blood was boiling. If the son of a bitch didn't have a damn gun on him, I'd beat the shit out of him.

"You'll be back," he laughed, shaking his head. "You always come back." He turned and made his way back down the driveway, where he climbed into his brand new Corvette.

"Not happening," I stated, watching him from my door to make sure he left my property.

Once he was gone, I sat heavily on the couch. Dropping my head into my hands, I wanted to scream at the part of my brain that kept saying, *"Just one more time. You'll be careful. Just go slow. Just a little line. It's not going to hurt you...Come on...You know you want it..."*

"Motherfucker!" I yelled, jumping to my feet. I made my way into the kitchen, scooping up my phone. I couldn't do this alone. I couldn't fall back into that lifestyle. I didn't want to die, and I knew damn good and well that if I did one more line of coke...I'd be dead.

"Taylor?" Mathew Gaines asked, answering on the first ring. Mathew's my sponsor, and when things get rough, he's the first person I call. I hurried to the bathroom off my kitchen and opened the baggie, spilling its contents into the toilet bowl, dropping the baggie in with it and hitting the handle to flush it down and out of my house.

"I...I need you," I gritted out, my eyes closed as I sat heavily on the couch. "My...my dealer came by the house."

"Ahh, man," he worried. "Did you...?"

"No!" I assured, relaxing when I heard him let out a heavy sigh. "I kicked him out, but I...I need to get out of here."

"I understand," he said. "Do you need me to come get you?"

"No," I replied. "I can come to you. I don't want to stay here any longer." This house held too many damn memories of the parties I had thrown, the drugs that flowed freely, and I was so fucking done. I couldn't stay in this house...I had to go before I did something that would forever change my life. I had to get help.

"Come on over, Taylor," he asserted, compassion in his voice. "You are welcome here as long as you need, brother."

"Thank you," I said gratefully, hanging up and packing a bag. I had to get my fucking shit straight. Maybe by then, Coraline would be able to forgive me, because right now, I needed to take care of myself.

CHAPTER 3

Coraline

Two Months Later

"I promise you, I won't kill him, Coraline," Kane sighed, pinching the bridge of his nose. "But I want to kill him." My cousin stood there shirtless, his massive collection of tattoos on display. His hair was the same jet black as my own. He kept his long and the sides shaved. Earlier in the day, I'd spiked his hair up into a wicked Mohawk that made him look even more dangerous than he normally did.

"I'm fine, it's over. I'd rather just go on with my life, Kane," I resolved, my voice only above a whisper. "Please, just let me do my job."

"Okay, but I'm here," he offered, reassuring me with a touch to my forearm. He stuck both hands into the pockets of his black denim jeans and kissed the top of my head.

"Okay," I acknowledged and grabbed a rolling case to take out to the stage.

Today was the last full day before Gabe went home to be with his wife. Taylor was going to take his spot on the rest of the tour for my cousin's band. I hadn't spoken to him since the night we'd spent on the island, and I'd stopped calling him the night I lost the baby. Like I told Kane, I just wanted to forget it and move on with my life.

I'd just run the lights around Kane's drum kit when I felt him enter the building. I was so attuned to Taylor Vaughn that I could feel him when he was near, and I hated it. We'd worked together many times over the years, and maybe that's why I knew the moment he stepped into the same room I was in. Maybe?

I heard the other roadies call out his name in excitement at his arrival and I gritted my teeth, climbing the scaffolding to hang a set of lights I'd set aside for just this moment. After this, I would be done with my portion of work and would make my way, very quickly, out to the bus.

"Cora," he called out.

"Hi, Taylor," I replied, turning away so I could focus on my job. Thankfully, Gabe came out of the backstage area and talked to him about some last minute things before he was scheduled to leave tomorrow.

After tonight's show, Gabe would head out, and Taylor would be the temporary guitarist for *Glory Days*. After this tour was over, Taylor would be off on his own tour with his band *Fatal Cross*. They'd be starting out overseas, and would be gone for only three weeks, before returning to the states. After that, he'd be on a six month excursion across the U.S., performing in smaller venues. His band wasn't at the caliber of my cousin's band, but *Fatal Cross* was quickly moving up the charts and would soon be selling out arenas if they kept gaining momentum with their music. As much as I disliked Taylor right now, I was happy for him and his success.

I glanced at him out of the corner of my eye and tried not to watch the way he walked or the way those jeans hugged his tight ass. Oh, he looked so much better than I remembered. He'd cut his long brown hair to a shorter style. The sides were shaved tight to his scalp and the top was so long that the ends brushed his strong cheekbones as it fell over his fiercely erotic green eyes. I swear he'd also put on about twenty pounds of muscle since I'd last seen him. His skin still looked as soft as I remembered it, though.

"*Fuck!*" I cursed under my breath.

"You alright up there?" Rita, one of our roadies, called out from below.

"Stupid lights," I shrugged and went back to work.

Once Taylor and Gabe were backstage, I hurried along with my work and came down so that I could make my escape from the stage and out to the bus. When I entered the backstage area, I groaned when I found Kane and Gabe talking near Taylor. Kane was glaring daggers at Taylor's back.

"You ready to go home and see your new baby?" I asked Gabe, trying to take their focus off of Taylor.

"Eighteen more hours," he sighed, glancing over his shoulder at Taylor. "Is everything okay? Should I be worried about leaving?"

"Everything's fine, Gabe," I lied. He looked between Kane and Taylor, and then to me. I shrugged and said my goodbyes, wishing him a safe trip home. "Give Brooklyn my best."

"Hey," Kane said, stopping me from leaving. "There's food in the back room, Cora. You should eat something while you can." God, he was so fucking protective. I really wished his wife was here so she could be under his watchful eye instead of me.

"Thanks," I nodded and made my way over to the room, Kane following behind me.

As I grabbed some food, Taylor walked in and ignored most of us, removing his laptop. Plugging it into the outlet on the far wall, he sat at a small bistro table that was set up with two chairs. He opened the lid and started typing away.

Instead of heading out to the safety of the bus like I'd originally wanted to do, I took to the corner of the couch and sat my plate on my crossed legs. Ash Martin, the lead singer of my cousin's band, took a seat next to me and smiled. "I'm going to have another baby."

"What?" I gasped, enveloping him in a hug. "I didn't know! Congrats, Big Papa!"

"Thanks," he smiled, looking pretty smug with his announcement. His wife was now pregnant with their third child. She was an amazing woman and perfect for the front man of *Glory Days*.

All this talk of babies had me happy for them, but made me want to pull my fucking hair out, what little I had. I kept the dark locks cut very short. I liked it that way so that I could work the rigorous task of getting the band set up and ready to perform for thousands of people every night. The thought of shaving it completely off was always an option, because after this tour, I'd either be bald from running my hands through it or prematurely gray from the stress.

Glancing over at Ash, I sighed heavily with the dark thoughts I'd been having lately. I wouldn't be a good mom. So, if I took a deep reality check, I'd realize that losing the baby was a good thing. I was only twenty-four and I had my whole life ahead of me. I wasn't quite ready to settle down and stay at home to raise a kid.

With my stomach churning, I dumped my plate and left the room. As I walked down the corridor to the rear exit of the building, I felt him behind me. I didn't turn or even slow down when I hit the door, pushing it open wide.

"Cora," Taylor said, calling out twice before I stopped once I had reached the bus.

"What, Taylor?" I sighed, turning around slowly to face him.

"Look," he began, running his fingers through his now shorter hair. His green eyes sparkled from the lights hanging above the door to the back of the venue. "I'm sorry I never called you back. It's just that I wanted to talk to you in person."

"Three months later?" I chided, glaring at his handsome face. Why the hell did my insides melt when he was so close? "Seriously?"

"I'm sorry," he pled, his green eyes masked with guilt. Puppy dog eyes. That's all he was doing, and I'd be dammed if I fell into that trap again.

"No," I protested. "*I'm* sorry. I'm sorry that what we did proved to me what a man whore you really are, and that I was nothing but a scratch you needed itched. Get the fuck away from me, Taylor Vaughn. I'm not your fucking whore."

Spinning on my heel, I stormed off toward the door of the bus, but Taylor obviously wasn't having any of that. A warm hand latched onto my upper arm, turning me around to face him. His guilty eyes were now deep emerald and very pissed off.

"You were *not* some fucking whore," he ranted. "And I swear to God, Coraline Maddox, if I *ever* hear you talk about yourself like that again, I will blister your ass to the point where you won't be able to sit down for a month."

"Leave me alone, Taylor," I sighed heavily, my shoulders slumping with exhaustion. I was so tired of replaying that night on the island over and over in my head.

"Never," he whispered, before pushing his weight into my body, causing my back to hit the cold exterior of the tour bus. His hand grasped my chin, holding it in place for his lips to capture them. I tried to struggle, but it was no use. Taylor was larger than me and the grip he had on my face was so dominating that I found myself not wanting him to release me. How fucked up was that?

The kiss was just as hot as I'd remembered. His tongue swept across my lip, and when I didn't open, he used his teeth to bite them. For a split second, I let myself get lost in his kiss, but I had to be strong. I had to stop this before it went too far…again.

"Please," I begged, turning my head to the left once he pulled back enough for us to take a breath. "Don't do this."

"Don't do what, Cora?" he whispered softly, landing one last press of his lips to the side of my neck.

"This," I stated. "We have to work together for a few weeks, then it's done…over, Taylor. I won't have sex with you again. Don't kiss me, either."

"And this is what you want?" he asked, looking into my eyes. I knew he was studying my face, watching for any sign of the truth. I couldn't lie worth a damn, and the traitorous tears pricking the backs of my eyes were a dead giveaway for what I was about to say.

"Yes, this is what I want," I lied, breaking away from him and rushing up the stairs to the bus. I went to my bunk and let the tears fall where no one could hear me cry.

I had to stay far away from that man, because Taylor Vaughn might just be my downfall.

CHAPTER 4

Taylor

Tasting Coraline Maddox again was like taking another line of cocaine into my system. She was addicting, and the taste was exquisite. I craved her more than I'd realized. If there was ever a female body that would make men go to war, that body would belong to Coraline Maddox. She was short, but curved in all the right places. Her breasts were huge and her hips flared perfectly for my large hands to grasp while I took her from behind. She had a little birthmark on the side of her right hip that looked like one half of a heart. I shivered when I remembered tasting that mark with my tongue.

As she ran up the steps on the bus, I heaved a deep breath and calmed my nerves. She was angry and had every right to be, because I had been a complete jerk to her. Not calling her was a jackass move, but I'd thought that a face to face explanation was due. It looked like she was not going to accept my apology anytime in the near future.

I wanted to call her…I really did. By the time she started calling me, I'd been heading back into the studio. I'd had a hard go of things right after returning from the studio that night and I'd been staying with my sponsor in Seattle for a few weeks. I'd lost my nerve to contact her and look where that got me…right in the damn doghouse. I'm lucky she didn't punch me in the fucking nuts.

Coraline Maddox wasn't a girly-girl. No, she was a badass bitch and a small part of me wanted her naked, screaming my name instead of orders. In fact, I wanted to tie her to my bed and listen to her calling out my name again and again.

Without a backwards glance, I tucked my hands in my pockets and headed for the back door to the venue. A security guard regarded me with cautioned eyes, but let me through without any problems after seeing the laminated pass attached to the key ring on my hip.

"Where's Cora?" Kane barked, as I rounded the corner. He looked worried, concerned.

"On the bus," I mumbled, walking past him. I didn't need to talk to her cousin and my friend. I just needed some alone time. I wanted to write music or punch myself. I hadn't decided yet.

Inside, I returned to the room where I had left my computer. I sat down and updated the *Fatal Cross* website. We were striking out on another tour in a few weeks. I would be meeting my band in London the final night of the *Glory Days* tour and the night before our tour kicked off. Our tour in the states would be long this time, almost six months, and I was pumped to get it started.

I had some unread emails from Cash regarding our new album and after replying to those, I looked up when I heard the opening band start up their set. I'd been writing and in my own little world for the better part of two hours.

I closed the laptop and slid it into the backpack at my feet. *Glory Days* was doing a meet and greet with their fans, so I pulled a hoodie over my head and ducked out the backdoor, escaping to the bus to store my things in the spare bunk.

The wind blew into my face as I stepped outside. Fall was approaching, and even though we were in Atlanta, they were experiencing unseasonably cool weather for September. I slipped my hands in my pockets and looked to my right, hoping Coraline was hanging out by the buses, but I was disappointed when she was nowhere to be found.

A commotion to my left had me turning. Some of the temporary help that wasn't part of the *Glory Days* crew were huddled together by the corner of the building. I knew immediately what the hell they were doing and I wanted no part of it. The stench of marijuana drifted across my face for a split second before I held my breath and climbed the stairs to the bus.

"Hey, Rita," I greeted, finding one of Ash's regular crew cleaning up the bus. "Who are those men out there?" There were three in all. A short skinny man, maybe in his mid-thirties with black hair, another man who was a bit taller with the same color hair, and an overweight man with dirty blonde hair all huddled at the corner of the building, passing around a joint as they laughed and talked.

"They are temporary help. They're on for several shows with us," she grumbled, gritting her teeth. "Assholes, if you ask me. Those bastards were giving Coraline and me a hard time a few hours before you got here. Made me want to take a bath." She tugged on the trash bag, pulling the full one out of the can and tying off the top.

"Wait," I demanded, stopping her from reaching for another bag. My heart sped in my chest. They'd approached Cora? And Rita? "What the hell did they say?"

"Nothing we don't hear every time we are on the road," she sighed, shaking out a new bag to line the can.

"Like what?" I pushed, demanding her to tell me.

"They think we are band whores," she offered, rolling her eyes. "One of those jerks actually offered Coraline money to suck him off."

"*What*?" I cursed. "Is she okay?"

"Oh, she's fine," Rita snorted out a laugh. The girl pushed a stray strand of hot pink hair behind her ear and pointed to the window, indicating the men. "See the one in the red and blue plaid shirt?"

"Yes," I growled, looking out the window of the bus.

"Do you see his black eye?" she asked.

"Well, not from here," I admitted, squinting to see the big guy across the parking lot. I couldn't miss which one she was talking about. The guy was huge, just barely larger than myself. Where I was muscled, this guy was overweight and he looked like he could use a bath.

"Well, Coraline Maddox gave him that shiner, honey," she laughed. "Don't think they'll be asking for anything from her again."

"Motherfucker," I swore, staring at the asshole that had bothered Cora. She had to defend herself. Hell, I knew she could, but she shouldn't have to do that. *Glory Days* had security guards everywhere. Where were they when Cora and Rita were being harassed? "I'm going to make sure they don't bother you guys again."

"Thanks, Taylor," Rita smiled. "But you don't have to do that. Cora and I pretty much take care of each other when we're on the road. We don't bother the guys much because they are too damn busy with everything else. If it ever got bad, we'd talk to Eric and let him know."

"I would hope so," I agreed. Eric was the band's head of security and he didn't take crap from anyone. I'd find him and let him know about the temps and their backstage antics. They wouldn't be working with us for much longer. And no one was going to touch Coraline Maddox as long as I had something to say about it.

CHAPTER 5

Coraline

"Damn, that man can play a fucking guitar," Rita purred, walking up next to me. We were standing at the side of the stage as Taylor played his first night filling in for Gabe. He was currently standing with his legs spread, his silver guitar slung low. The back of the guitar laid against his upper thigh as he strummed the thing with expert precision. His head was thrown back and his eyes were closed as he played the song as if he'd written the music himself. Fuck! He was hot as hell.

"Yes, he can," I cleared my throat and admitted truthfully. The song ended and I watched as the lights dimmed, allowing everyone to get into their spots for the next song. Ash ran up the scaffolding to the ledge behind Kane's drum kit. He looked over at me and I gave Kane a thumbs up, letting them know they were all set to begin the next song. I keyed the mic, letting the sound guy know to start the prerecorded instrumental opening for the song.

"He also can't keep his eyes off of you," she chuckled, nudging me with her shoulder.

"What?" I blushed, spinning around so she wouldn't see the obvious lust I had in my eyes. "What the hell are you talking about?"

"Oh, Cora," she laughed, almost in a scolding manner. I glanced over my shoulder when she let out an unladylike snort. "You know damn good and well that man cannot stop looking at you. You look at him when you think no one is looking, too. You just need to hit that shit and get it out of your system."

"No," I objected, averting my eyes. "I don't."

I didn't know if she heard me or not, but I had to get the fuck out of there. I couldn't watch him play any longer. I had to get my head on straight, because in about twenty minutes, it would be time to tear down the stage and load up the trucks. The last thing I need was to have amorous thoughts of the sexy guitarist causing me to slack on my job.

I heard the roar of the crowd as they finished the last song in the set. I rushed back to the steps at the side of the stage and handed them all towels to wipe off the copious amounts of sweat they'd produced from exerting themselves so much on stage.

Ash, *Glory Days'* lead singer, tossed his sweat soaked shirt at me and I caught it before he rushed back on stage for their encore. Taylor cast a glance over his shoulder and frowned at something over my head as he followed the guys back up the stairs.

I groaned as I looked over my shoulder at the men that helped with tear down. The one who'd propositioned me earlier in the day was standing amongst his friends, glaring at me with a hatred I was used to seeing from guys I'd put in their place.

The guy, Doug, sneered at me one last time before turning his back so he could line up cases to put the equipment in after the show. I noticed the black eye was getting more and more pronounced since I'd decked him when he asked me to give him a blowjob. The asshole didn't take too kindly to my refusal.

As the lights went down, I stood waiting for the guys to walk off stage. Ash and Reed, the bassist, handed me their ear pieces and patted me on the shoulder. I still needed to let Ash know about the problem I had with the temporary help, but it could wait. I didn't want to bother him when he was busy. My job was to keep them on schedule, and throwing a wrench into this well-oiled machine could very well screw up their entire tour. These guys needed to concentrate on their performances, not a small altercation with their crew. I was in charge, and it was my job to deal with the people who worked for the band. I just couldn't bother Ash with that asshole's filthy mouth at the moment. We had a job to do.

"Move, bitch," Doug grunted, pushing me out of his way with a heavy shoulder. I stumbled into a solid chest, a silver guitar glinting in my periphery.

"What the fuck?" Taylor snarled, wrapping a protective arm around the top of my shoulders. I pushed off of him quickly and cringed from the hatred rolling off of his features. He slipped his guitar strap over his head and handed the guitar to Rita, who was standing there glaring at Doug. Taylor stepped right up into the jerk's private space and snarled, "Did that black eye not teach you some manners?"

"Taylor," I gasped, pulling on his forearm to stop him from going after the guy. "Please, don't."

"Don't?" he scoffed, glaring at me like I had three heads. The noise of the crowd drowned out my growl of embarrassment. I'd already taken care of this guy. Now, Taylor had to put his two cents worth in on a subject that should've been closed when I'd punched the guy.

"I took care of it," I barked, glancing at Doug, who hadn't backed down a bit since Taylor had stepped into our confrontation. Taylor was not small, not even when he was on drugs. He'd obviously been working out since the last time I saw him, because he didn't have an ounce of fat on his bulky form. He was beautiful before…now he's just stunning.

"Doesn't look like it to me," he snarled, swiveling around to point a finger in Doug's chest. I smirked at the fear that flashed across Doug's face, but it was quickly replaced with anger…at me. "You do *not* talk to her or any other woman like you did earlier. I won't stand for it. Do your fucking job or hit the road. Got me?"

How the hell did he know what happened earlier? I had my answer when I looked at Rita and she had the gall to look apologetic. Clenching my teeth, I spun on my heel and headed for the stage, leaving them to argue. I didn't like issues on the crew, and I knew my cousin would fire Doug or anyone else who caused problems. It was my job to handle this shit, but it looked like Taylor was taking it upon himself to reinforce that with the temporary help.

Climbing the scaffolding, I distanced myself from everyone, plugging in my headphones and ignoring the people below me. I didn't need to talk to Taylor, or Rita, or anyone else for that matter. We had only two hours to get this completely torn down and loaded up before it was time to head out to Dallas.

My hands shook as I worked, because I'd caught sight of Taylor standing off the side of the stage, watching me. He needed to stop. I couldn't get involved with him, and that damn kiss a few days ago burned me from the inside out.

Thankfully, Ash came around and pulled him backstage for something. Hell, anything they were doing was better than him being around me. I'd been hurt once by him, and I refused to be his whore. He'd made our one night stand perfectly clear when he wouldn't return my calls.

It took about an hour and a half for the complete teardown of the stage. The regular staff that worked for *Glory Days* took over for me while I ran out to the bus to make sure the guys were all set to leave. I knew he'd be on the bus, but I had a job to do. Of course, I kept telling myself that I was doing my job and not excited at all to see him. I was an idiot and knew that any close proximity to Taylor Vaughn was not in my best interest.

It was dark and the large lights overhead hummed as I exited the building. The noise was welcomed for the short time it took me to get to the bus. I knocked on the bus door and waited for their driver to open the door.

"Hey, Cora," Sam smiled, setting his book on his lap.

"Are they all set?" I asked, nodding toward the back.

"Yeah, they're on the phone with their wives," he laughed, shaking his head. "Never thought I'd see these guys settle down, but it happened."

"I'm happy for them," I admitted.

"When are you going to find a nice young man to knock you off your feet, young lady?" he questioned.

"I'm waiting for your missus to give you up, Sam," I winked, refusing to think of Taylor. "You know you are the only man to hold my heart." I pinched his cheek, before planting a kiss to his forehead.

"A girl after my own heart," he blushed, shaking his head.

"Let me check on them and we will head out in an hour," I said, pushing open the curtain separating the driver's seat and the living area of their bus. "Hey, guys."

"Cora," they answered in unison.

Ash was sitting at the small table with his laptop opened. He was the father figure the whole band needed and was the brains behind the number one rock band in recent history. Ash Martin was a powerful man and one hell of a singer. He smiled warmly at me as I took a seat on the leather couch next to my cousin.

"We about ready to head out?" Ash asked, pushing his sun-kissed blonde hair out of his sparkling green eyes.

"I'm about to crash," Kane yawned, draping an arm across my shoulders. I turned my head and looked into hazel eyes that matched my own. Our fathers were brothers and total opposites. Kane's parents were very religious and straight laced, whereas my father would rather find his religion at the bottom of a whiskey bottle.

"When we get to Dallas tomorrow, you guys have an interview at the rock station. You're scheduled to be there at noon," I rattled off, handing Ash a sheet of paper with the details printed out. I always took care of them by providing a schedule for each city, letting them know when they had free time to do things on their own. I tried not to book them on too many appearances because I didn't want to burn them out.

"I really don't know what I would do without you some days, Cora," Ash beamed, looking over the schedule.

"I told you I was going to be the best damn tour manager slash roadie extraordinaire you'd ever seen," I giggled. That laugh died in my throat when Taylor came out of the bunk area.

A lump formed in my throat, causing me to swallow two or three times...hard. Taylor had stopped in his tracks and just stared in my direction. He was shirtless, his hair was slicked back away from his face and his black lounge pants hung dangerously low across his hips. The deep V shaped muscle peeking out of said pants caught my eye as I tracked up his tanned chest. The barbells pierced through his nipples sparkled when the light over his head caught them just right. He had a cross tattoo down the left side of his ribcage that was simple, yet beautiful. There was no color in the cross; only a deep black shading within the outline. I shivered when I remembered tracing it with my tongue.

"Okay," I jumped up, stumbling over Kane's feet. He steadied me and frowned, but didn't say anything. "I'll see you guys in Dallas. Call me if you need anything."

I said a quick goodbye to Sam and hurried down the stairs. I walked at a fast pace, pulling the much needed fresh air into my lungs. I tried not to admit that I'd smelled his unique scent on that bus, but I was also lying to myself. I'd almost made it to the back door of the arena when I heard his voice.

"Cora," Taylor called out. The hairs on the back of my neck were tingling in warning, but my heart was saying to just jump in his arms and let him know…everything.

What good would that do anyway, really? He didn't need to have something thrown in his face that he had no control over. Oh, who was I kidding? I wanted to cry and scream and throw shit in his fucking face!

"What?" I barked, exasperated. My hand was on the door. All I had to do was pull. If I did, then I could escape to some dark corner in the arena and maybe, just maybe, I'd get out of his sight until the bus left.

"Talk to me," he pleaded. He almost sounded depressed. "What did I do wrong?"

"Really?" I spat, spinning around to glare daggers at him. He was closer than I'd thought and my face was only inches from his broad chest. *Damn, he smells amazing!* The compulsion to bolt was long forgotten. "You have to ask me that?" Was he that stupid?

"Other than not calling you?" he sighed, looking guilty as hell. "We have to work together, Cora. I've said that I was sorry. I had…I was unable to talk to you."

"I don't care, Taylor," I stressed, clenching my teeth to keep the tears at bay. "It's over. I just want to get the next six shows over and then you can go overseas. After this tour is over, we are done."

"So, that's it?" he pouted, but his green eyes were shadowed by guilt. I had to look away from him or I'd give in and let him touch me.

My skin ached to be held in his arms again…to let go of the control I had on my life.

"That's it, Taylor," I answered, pulling the door open and leaving him standing there.

I barely made it to the ladies restroom before the tears rolled down my face.

Dallas was always fun. Rita and I, along with some of the crew, usually took off for a few hours of downtime after the show. We'd be staying in town tonight, before heading to New Mexico the next afternoon. The show had just finished and I was in a hurry to get out of the building and away from Taylor.

"Cora," Rita called out.

"Yeah?" I asked, looking down from my perch in the scaffolding. "What's up?"

"Hurry the hell up! We are going to be left behind!" she laughed and wagged her eyebrows. She was up to something and I'm sure it had to do with Taylor. I really wished she'd give up on this hit it or quit it campaign she'd adopted over the past few days.

"Okay," I nodded. "Give me fifteen!"

"I'll be ready," she smiled, throwing a wink over her shoulder as she hopped off the stage.

I hurried along, gathering the last of the equipment, rushing out to the trailer to lock things up. A fast shower and change of clothes later, I was bouncing on the tips of my toes as Rita, Kane, and I piled into the SUV Eric had pulled around by the crew's bus.

"I knew you needed a night out," Kane paused. He'd taken it upon himself to go with us to the club, saying he only wanted to make sure we were safe. I wasn't going to complain, because he was alone and Taylor was nowhere to be found. It was time to let my hair down.

Lights flashed in time to the deep bass of the song that was currently playing as we approached the doors. Eric and Kane stood on the outside of our little group, keeping Rita and I wedged between them. I saw Rita's eyes roaming up and down my cousin's security and she blushed when she realized I'd caught her in the act.

"Oh, shush," she giggled. "Can't blame a girl for looking."

"Huh?" Kane asked, raising his voice over the music.

"Nothing," Rita and I said in unison, bursting out into an obnoxious laughter when we looked up to see both men looking clueless.

Once the bouncer at the door saw Kane, we were waved to the front of the line, entering the building in a rush. Eric stopped and spoke to one of the men, shaking his hand as he turned to escort us to a set of stairs. We'd visited this place before. The upstairs area circled the building, a half wall with brass railing, giving a loft like appeal to the place.

Kane pulled out a chair for me and waved to a passing waitress. I ordered a mixed drink while the others ordered a pitcher of beer. Kane leaned back in his seat and smiled warmly at me, silently telling me that tonight was my night to relax and enjoy myself.

My cousin and I were so close that we didn't need words to express ourselves. I appreciated him for doing this, and the smile that lit up my face was thanks enough for what he'd done. He gave me a chance to let it all go.

Grabbing Rita, we laughed loudly as we made our way to the dance floor. Once there, I glanced over my shoulder to see Kane and Eric standing up at the railing, watching our every move. It'd been a few years since his wife had almost been drugged at a club similar to this one, and I knew he wouldn't let anything happen to us.

"Your cousin is my favorite person," Rita laughed, throwing her hands in the air and shaking her ass to the song that was pumping heavily through the sound system.

"He's a good man," I admitted, smiling to myself.

"That he is," she replied, grabbing my hand and spinning me around like a ballerina. I threw my head back and laughed loudly. Tonight was going to be amazing, because I wouldn't let it be any other way.

A new song started and I let myself get lost in the music, feeling tiny beads of sweat roll down my spine. More people crowded on the floor, causing Rita and I to push closer together. She laughed when I threw my hands in the air and let her lean against my chest so that we could dance together. A few men looked at us with lust in their eyes, but they didn't approach. I was free to flirt and even dance with them, but I was here for myself...not to find a date.

As the night went on, Rita and I made several trips to the table to have drinks and chat with Kane, who promised he was enjoying himself even though he wasn't down there with us. He'd calmed down a lot since he got married and had children. Seeing him happy and relaxed was the best feeling in the world. I was truly happy for him.

"One more dance?" Rita begged. It was going on two in the morning and our time was coming to a close. I noticed Kane pull his phone out of his back pocket and frown at something on the screen. He quickly schooled his features and took a long pull off of his beer.

"I think two more," I smirked, feeling the warmth from my own drinks flowing through my body. I wasn't drunk, but the buzz I had left me a bit wobbly on my feet.

"You alright?" Kane asked, steadying me when my foot caught the leg of his chair. Thankfully, I didn't face plant and make a fool of myself.

"Yes, sir," I giggled, feeling a little more buzzed than when I was sitting down.

Rita and I took off for the stairs and giggled as we found our way back to the floor. The lights had doubled in strength and I squinted my eyes to be able to see where I was dancing. Following Rita, we made our way to the middle where there was a group of people grinding against each other, their hands thrown in the air.

Large hands slid over my hips and I felt a hard body mold itself to my back. I closed my eyes, savoring the feel of a man's strength against my small body. My arms lifted in the air and hooked around the back of his neck, letting his face settle against my neck. My eyes were still closed and I absorbed the feel of his touch for as long as I could before I needed to pull away.

I didn't want to pull away. That was the problem, wasn't it? I wanted him to hold me, protect me, and comfort me. I needed his strength for those times when I couldn't be strong. Those few moments in my life when I wanted to just let go…let someone else call the shots for me. Was that too much to ask? Was it too much to hope for, coming from a woman who prided herself on her independence?

I just wanted to give that control over to one person…

And as I opened my eyes, there on that packed dance floor, I saw exactly who I wanted holding me. He was standing about ten feet in front of me, his eyes dark with anger. I felt hands gliding up my sides, making quick work toward the sides of my breasts.

As the music stopped, I heard a deathly growl come from Taylor, just as I realized the man who was touching me wasn't the man I wanted.

"Coraline!" Kane called out from my right. As I turned my head, I saw panic in his features. My alcohol fueled brain was slow to understand that he was trying to get me away and out from between Taylor and the man who'd basically felt me up on the dance floor.

Scrambling backwards, I must've tangled my feet together, because I felt myself falling, just as the strange man reached out, softly grabbing the tops of my arms to set me upright.

"Are you okay, doll?" he asked. Even with my blurry eyes, I noticed he was very good looking. His long dark hair touched his shoulders and his green eyes were soft. He was large, but not as large as the man who'd just rushed up to pull me behind his large frame.

"Taylor," I warned. Well, it sounded slurred to my ears, and I'm pretty sure the rolling of my stomach had nothing to do with being moved around so quickly and everything to do with the six mixed drinks I'd consumed. Or was it seven?

"Go with your cousin," Taylor warned, his eyes never leaving the man who'd been dancing with me. "Now, Cora!"

"No," I barked, locking my knees to keep me upright. "No, you don't get to do this, Taylor."

"The fuck I don't," he growled. "He had his fucking hands on you."

"And?" I pressed, knowing damn well I was poking the beast. That beast was about to lay down a path of destruction, but I just couldn't keep my fucking mouth shut. "Maybe I *wanted* to dance with him?"

"Excuse me?" Taylor cursed, turning around to glare daggers at me instead of the sexy, dancing man. I looked over Taylor's shoulder at the man in question and gave him my best drunken flirty smile. "Coraline...now would *not* be the best time to push me."

"Go back to the bus, Taylor," I said, sidestepping when he made a move to reach for my hand. I was proud of myself for not stumbling. Placing my hands on my hips I continued to glare at him. "Get the fuck away from me, Taylor!"

"Come on, doll," the guy said. "Let me take you to the bar for another drink."

"Oh, shit," Rita gasped.

Eric and Kane made a grab for Taylor, pulling him back from mauling the guy. It took both men to drag him off of the dance floor. I watched as Taylor jerked to the right, dislodging himself from my cousin and his security guard.

"It may be best if you get the hell out of here," I said, looking over my shoulder at the guy who now had a target on his head. "Go!" He didn't need to be told a third time. I sighed heavily when he disappeared into the crowd that had gathered around us.

The music continued, but there was no one dancing. Everyone had pulled out their cell phones and were patiently waiting for the guitarist for *Fatal Cross* to do something that would have him splashed across every gossip rag in the country before noon.

My hand was grabbed and I found myself being pulled out of the club, Rita was hot on my tail. Taylor didn't stop until we reached the SUV, picking me up and tossing me into the seat. I shook my head at Kane when he opened his mouth to speak. This was my issue to take care of, and as soon as we got to the bus, I'd remind him to stay the hell away from me.

The ride to the bus was quiet, Taylor continued to fume next to me in the seat. Rita and Kane kept giving me sideways glances as I kept my arms folded across my chest. My stomach knotted and I had to swallow a few times to keep from emptying my stomach in the floorboard of the truck.

As soon as we arrived, Rita hopped out of the vehicle first, standing just outside the door in case I needed her help. I gave her a short nod, silently telling her I would be okay. Kane pulled me into a hug and I could tell he was unsure of what to say or do. "Go on the bus, Kane. I got this."

"You need to talk to him," he whispered, kissing my temple before walking away.

Gritting my teeth, I decided that now wasn't the time to get into an argument with Taylor. I'd been drinking and I knew that I would say something I'd later regret, but he wasn't going to let me just crawl out to the bus and lick my wounds.

"So, were you going to go home with that guy?" he snarled.

"Oh, you think that highly of me?" I gasped. "Fuck you, Taylor."

"I can't believe you were that irresponsible," he yelled. "How much did you have to drink?"

"That's none of your business," I argued, averting my eyes. I couldn't look at him when he was this angry. I didn't like it at all. "I wasn't in any trouble. Kane and Eric were close…and what does it matter to you? We are not together, Taylor. You have no claim on me."

"Oh," he chuckled, but not in humor. "You are mine, Coraline Maddox, and you damn well know that. The next man who touches you is a dead motherfucker. You're lucky I didn't kill that son of a bitch for molesting you in that club."

"I. Am. Not. Yours!" I yelled. It was my turn to get angry. "You gave up that right when you refused to call me back…when you decided that you'd wait almost three months to talk to me! Get the hell away from me, Taylor, and do not ever throw your claim on me like that again."

I turned and ran for the bus, ignoring his growl of frustration, but I didn't miss the words he shouted at my retreating back.

"Damn it, Coraline. You are mine!"

God, I think I might be sick.

CHAPTER 6

Taylor

It'd been two shows since she'd basically run away from me, saying she wanted nothing to do with me. I'd really fucked up, and I'd apologized until I was blue in the face. I shouldn't have acted like a raging beast in that club, but seeing that asshole with his hands on her made me murderous.

We'd just come back from an interview at the local radio station in Phoenix. Even though I was only filling in for Gabe, *Glory Days* asked me to go with them to do the interview. It was good press for my band, *Fatal Cross*, and I wasn't going to tell them I couldn't go. Ash and the guys had always helped us out from the first time we'd met. Hell, without them, we wouldn't be where we were today.

The guys headed for the bus so that they could call home while they had an hour or two to spare. I, on the other hand, looped around toward the back of the arena to see if I could get a glimpse of the woman who haunted my dreams.

"Where the hell is Doug?" Rita growled, looking into one of the closed rooms just inside the entrance. She shut the door with a loud bang and turned toward me with a scowl on her face. Her pink hair was in disarray and I swear she looked like she was ready to crack.

"What the hell is going on?" I demanded, feeling a sense of dread and worry fall over my senses. Something wasn't right...I could feel it. My heart raced in my chest, pounding in my ears. My senses were all over the radar. Even the backstage area felt...weird.

"The temp crew is running behind because that jackass hasn't shown up and we are so far behind, it'll be a miracle if we get everything set up to start on time tonight," she said, running her fingers through her hot pink hair.

"Where's Coraline?" I growled, knowing for sure that something wasn't right when I heard her curse.

"Oh, shit," she gasped, looking around the area. I didn't have to ask, but she said it anyway. "I haven't seen her for at least an hour. You don't think?"

"Fuck," I swore, my heart dipping to my stomach. I couldn't even answer her question, because I knew something was terribly wrong. "Find Eric!" I pushed her carefully toward the back door. Rita hauled ass outside to find *Glory Days'* head of security while I searched the venue.

My feet pounded on the hard concrete floor. My heart thundered in my ears so loudly that I was sure it was echoing off the cinderblock walls. The scent of pine and bleach assaulted me as I followed the corridor around the backstage area. With each torturous step, I prayed I'd find her…soon.

I called her name as I checked each room. There were doors every ten to fifteen feet, most of them nothing more than empty, unused areas. Some were used for storage, others as dressing rooms for the entertainers.

If Doug was going to get revenge on Cora for that black eye she gave him, then today would've been a great day to do it because security and her cousin were away for a few hours. With everyone out of sight, then he could've hurt her…or worse.

I didn't want to think about the "or worse" part.

"Taylor," Kane called out, rushing to my side. "Have you found her?" Kane Maddox loved his baby cousin more than any siblings I'd ever seen. That man would give his life for hers, and I knew exactly how he felt. Coraline Maddox had weaved her way into my heart, body, and soul, and there was no way in hell I was going to sit back and let her be hurt.

"No, man," I choked, swallowing tears of rage. I needed to calm the fuck down, because she just *had* to be okay…wherever she was.

I slammed into one of the women's restrooms, not caring if there were any girls in there. I slapped my hand on each and every stall door. My heart held in my throat as each one revealed an empty space. The lights overhead hummed quietly as the heartbeat in my ears tried to overpower every other sound in the room.

"She has to be okay," I whispered, not thinking anyone would hear me.

"She better be," Kane growled, placing a calming hand on my shoulder. "We will find her."

"I won't be able to live with myself if something happened to her and I wasn't here to protect her," I vowed, not caring if he realized that I'd just laid some unwritten claim on his cousin. She *was* mine and always would be; no matter what she thought. From the harsh scowl on his face, I didn't think Kane missed the possessive tone to my words, either.

"You really do care about her?" he inquired with a raised brow.

"More than my own life," I promised, pushing open the janitor's closet at the end of the hallway. What I found there had me crying out in sheer rage. "Cora!"

"Cora!" Kane wailed, falling to his knees next to me.

She was beaten and bloody. Her wrists were turning black and blue from someone holding them with force. Blood trickled out of her nose and her head had a huge purple lump forming on her left side.

I immediately reached for her neck, praying I'd find a pulse. "She's alive," I yelled, hearing Kane on the phone with someone, hopefully the paramedics.

"See if you can wake her," Kane ordered, obviously relaying the dispatcher's request.

"Come on, baby girl," I cooed, stroking the side of her face that was undamaged. "When I find that son of a bitch, I'm going to kill him."

Cora wore a pair of jeans and a purple tank top. Her skin felt cold to the touch, so I stripped off my leather jacket and laid it carefully across her upper body. I wanted nothing more than to pull her into my arms and hold her tight, promising her no one would ever harm her again.

"Don't move her," Kane barked. I guess I'd reached for her without thought. "The ambulance should be here any second." I had to gently lay her back on the cold concrete floor, against all of my instincts to cradle her in my arms.

Feeling her tiny body in my arms, I said a silent prayer of gratitude that I'd found her and that she was alive. I also vowed vengeance against the asshole who'd dared to put his hands on her.

Looking up, I saw the concrete floor littered with specks of green. Kane followed my gaze and cursed out loud, but I already knew what it was. Marijuana was scattered all over the floor by a table that was on its side. Small, clear plastic bags were among the mess.

"She walked in on him," I surmised, vibrating harshly with anger. "He could've fucking killed her, Kane!" The son of a bitch was dealing drugs!

"I know," he barked. "I fucking know this! I swear to God, if she's okay, I'm going to blister her ass."

"Not if I do it first," I promised.

Commotion behind us had my eyes turning to see Ash, Reed, and Eric barging through the door. A look of agony crossed each man's features. Reed cursed loudly, pulling at his long hair. Ash fell to his knees beside me and leaned over her head like he was assessing her injuries.

"Who did this?" he demanded, looking around the room.

"It was Doug," Rita announced, entering the room. "I *know* it was him!"

"Whoa, wait a minute," Ash said, holding up one hand. "What the hell is going on? Why do you think Doug did this?"

Rita spat out the story of Doug talking to Cora and her like band whores, wanting to pay Cora for a blowjob. Cora didn't take to kindly to his advances, punching him in the eye. Rita told Ash that they didn't say anything to any of them, because the guys had more things to worry about that a confrontation with their crew. I'd already heard this story, but it still sent a new wave a fury through my veins.

"You do not *ever* think that we are too busy for the crew, Rita," Ash admonished. "This is something that we need to know about. This isn't something small! This is serious!"

Ash's words were cut short when Coraline moaned, trying to roll to one side. I immediately leaned over her body so that I was in her line of sight, taking her face gently between my hands and holding her completely still.

"Shh, baby girl, don't move," I commanded, placing a bit of demand into my voice, but not enough to scare her. She was so tiny on a normal day, but at the moment, she looked even more fragile. I wiped a tear that leaked out of her right eye when she blinked rapidly.

"T...Taylor," she rasped, trying to use the back of her hand to wipe at her bloody nose. I grabbed a tissue that someone had thrust in my face, gently wiping away the red stain from her soft skin.

"I've got you, Cora," I told her, wiping one last spot on her cheek. "You're safe and an ambulance is coming."

"No, I'm fine," she groaned, gritting her teeth. When she tried to sit up, I pushed gently on her shoulder to keep her on the ground.

"*No*," I growled. "Stay put. You are going to the hospital and you will get checked out by a doctor."

"Ow," she moaned, throwing her hand over her eyes. I didn't like how pale her skin looked and I sure as hell didn't want to keep her on the cold concrete floor.

When I tucked my jacket around her body, I felt her flinch away from my touch and that shattered my heart more than I ever thought possible. I bowed my head in defeat. I'd obviously hurt this woman and it was killing me that she wouldn't talk to me. Now, she was broken and bleeding on the floor and wouldn't even accept the comforting touch I so desperately wanted to give her.

The paramedics arrived along with two officers before Cora could protest. Rita stepped out of the room with one of the police officers to give a statement and a description of Doug. I had to move away from Cora as the paramedics started questioning her as to what happened.

"I was coming off the stage," she started, wincing when the paramedic stuck the needle in her arm to start an IV. "I was heading for the bathroom when I heard something coming from this room. I opened the door and found him distributing bags of weed into smaller ones. I confronted him and he pushed me, knocking the table over. The stuff went everywhere and he went crazy. He…he grabbed me and punched me in the side of the head. That's all I remember."

"Were you violated, ma'am?" the second paramedic asked, writing information down on a clipboard. My nostrils flared at his question. Rage boiled deep in my bones, and I clenched my hands at my sides, concentrating on keeping myself calm. Doug was a dead man. As soon as I knew she was okay, I would find the asshole myself. The police better hope they find him first. The only reason why I wasn't losing my shit was because she was still fully clothed.

"I don't think so," she shivered, her eyes glancing my way. She quickly looked away and locked eyes with the guy prepping her for the ride to the hospital. "Like I said, I don't remember much."

"I need some information," he began. "What is your full name?"

"Coraline Marie Maddox," she replied.

"Height and weight?" he asked.

"Five-three," she answered, but paused when the other man touched her ribs. "Ow, that fucking hurts!"

"Sorry, ma'am," he said quickly. I had to bite my lip to keep from smiling. My girl was a tough one. I was surprised she didn't punch the guy in the throat.

"Weight and age?" the guy with the clipboard continued.

"One-ten and I'm twenty-four," she yawned.

"She may have a concussion," he whispered, looking over at us as we stood out of the way, but close enough to be at her side in an instant.

They continued by strapping a neck brace on her and then put her on a backboard, before carefully moving her on to a stretcher. Kane and I immediately went to her side once they tightened the belt around her waist.

"Taylor and I will be right behind the ambulance," Kane informed her, taking one of her tiny hands.

"No," she protested, wincing when she squirmed on the stretcher. I wouldn't be surprised if she had a cracked rib. The thought made me even more murderous. "Stay here. You have a meet and greet in two hours. You can't miss that!"

"Shut up, Coraline," Kane barked, leaning in closer to her face. "You are officially off duty. If I have to, I will fire your stubborn ass until you are better."

"Kane," she warned, glaring at him from her position strapped to the stretcher. Even tied up, Coraline Maddox couldn't curb her tongue.

"No," I interrupted, stepping up beside her as the paramedics wheeled her through the corridor and out to the ambulance. "You *will* not worry about this. Everything will work out."

"Rita?" Cora called out. Rita hurried to her side next to Kane.

"What do you need me to do, Cora?" she asked, tears building in the corners of her eyes, but she didn't let them fall. Rita was just as tough as Cora, but she was a little softer around the edges.

"The radio station will be here at six to set up," she explained, spouting off orders like a drill sergeant. "Make sure the guys are in and out of there on time."

"I've got this," Rita promised, clasping Cora's hand. "Go get checked out. I'll take care of the guys."

"Okay," Cora sighed, heavily. I didn't miss the wince of pain when the stretcher bumped over a rough patch in the parking lot. "Okay."

The next twenty minutes were a blur of motion. We were whisked away in the SUV Eric had rented to get us to and from the radio station. Kane sat next to me in the backseat, on the phone, cursing when he couldn't get an answer from whomever he was calling. I watched as the scenery passed by the windows in a blur. I was too worried to pay attention to where we were going. I trusted Eric to get us to the hospital and to Cora.

"Her fucking father is nowhere to be found," he cursed...again. "My dad said that he'd try and get ahold of him, but I doubt we will hear from him."

"So, what's up with that?" I asked, raising a brow. Kane was steadily calling and calling her father, cursing when it went to voicemail. "Her dad out of the picture?"

"He's a drunk," Kane remarked, shaking his head at a bad memory. "After Cora's mom died, he started drinking and would run off for days, leaving her home alone. I was older than her by seven years, and ended up staying at her place when her dad took off. I had to make sure she was fed and at school every morning. I've practically raised that girl."

"What an asshole," I growled. "She doesn't need to worry about him. I...we can take care of her." Kane didn't comment on my slip of the tongue when referring to taking care of Coraline, but there was no mistaking the flare of his nostrils at what I'd said.

"You better not hurt her again," Kane warned, clenching his fists. He narrowed his eyes in my direction, making his silent threat more menacing. I was sure that Kane Maddox would go to blows if anyone disrespected his cousin in any way.

"Again?" I asked, turning in my seat. I looked at him, confused. What the hell was he saying about me hurting her? I knew he wasn't talking about physically, because I'd cut off my own arm before ever laying a hand on a woman, especially Cora.

"Yes, again," he ground out, still glaring at me. He was obviously angry at me for not calling her. I shouldn't be surprised that she'd talked to him about our time on the island. They were very close and obviously didn't keep secrets from each other.

"She won't talk to me…won't tell me what the hell is going on, Kane," I complained, completely frustrated.

"She hasn't talked to you...since?" he asked, shock on his face. He frowned at his own thoughts, and I wanted to scream at him to tell me what the hell was going on with her.

"No," I sighed. The last thing I wanted to do was to bring up what happened between us to her cousin, but *fuck*...I had to know what the hell was going on with her. "We hooked up on the island and she tried to call me, but I was..."

"Was what?" he demanded. "Were you with someone else?"

"No, not like that," I said, preparing myself to spill the beans, but that never came, because Eric announced that we'd arrived at the emergency room.

"We will talk about this later," Kane warned. "My only worry is Coraline right now."

"She is my only concern, too," I responded, nodding my agreement as I hurried to her bedside.

CHAPTER 7

Coraline

Sounds irritated my ears and the light shining in my face made my head hurt so much that I wanted to claw my eyes out with a dull fork. The paramedics helped the nurses move me off of the stretcher I'd been brought in on just a few minutes ago.

"Ms. Maddox?" a male voice said. Opening my eyes, I blinked rapidly, then groaned from the brain splitting pain to the backs of my peepers. "How much pain are you in?"

"That light needs to be doused, doc," I cursed. "My head feels like it was used as a bowling ball."

"I need to take a look in your eyes, ma'am," he said, politely. "Then I'll dim the lights for you, but we are going to have to run some tests. I think you may have a concussion."

Yeah, no shit, Sherlock! "Okay, thank you," I murmured, not even trying to smile.

That douche-canoe Doug was a fucking dead man if I ever got my hands on him. I'd been so careful to watch out for him, and the split second I let my guard down, he attacked me.

"Did they catch this Doug? The one that did this to you?" the doc questioned.

"Did I say that aloud?" *Oops!* My brain sometimes spills out shit that I'm thinking. I hoped I didn't offend anyone.

"It's okay, Ms. Maddox," he smiled, once I opened my eyes and actually got a glimpse of the good doctor. He was older, closer to my father's age. His hair was a dark brown and his eyes held mine as he continued. "My name is Dr. Baker. I will be running some tests on you to see what's going on after your attack. The police are here to ask you a few questions after we are done. I need to know if you were sexually assaulted."

"Hell, no," I growled. "I would've killed the son of a bitch."

"I wouldn't have stopped you if he did," the doc nodded. "Let's get you looked at."

For the next ten minutes, Dr. Baker checked all of my reflexes and looked over every inch of my body after I was put into a hospital gown that barely covered my modesty. Since I didn't have much of that, it really didn't matter to me what the hell they dressed me in, so long as I was able to get the hell out of here in the next hour.

"I'm really going to be okay," I encouraged, hoping to hurry him along. "I just took a nasty bump on the head. I'll be fine in a few days."

"Your cousin is in the waiting room," a nurse announced as she walked into the room.

"I need to get back to the stadium," I demanded. "I have a job to do."

"Your cousin also said to take care of you first, and to tell you that you were fired if you didn't get checked out," she smiled, a faint blush dusted the tops of her cheekbones. I rolled my eyes at the women getting flustered by my cousin and his bandmates. They were all very good looking and they were also very attached to women I loved and respected. I was in no mood to defend them against fans at the hospital.

"Arg," I snarled, throwing my wrist over my face. Shielding my eyes, I listened to the doctor give orders for my care. When he pressed the knot on the side of my face, I gasped out in pain. The cursing I gave the doctor would've made a sailor blush, but damn it…that hurt.

I was wheeled back for x-rays, CT scans, and a host of other imaging to make sure my brain was functioning properly. They ended up giving me an internal exam to make sure I wasn't raped. By the time it was all said and done, I was given the okay to be released, but was informed that I had a slight concussion. I was to be watched overnight for any weird changes.

Finally, I was told to dress back into the clothes I was wearing when I arrived at the hospital. A knock on the door had me straightening my shirt a little faster before telling whoever it was that I was decent.

My heart lurched in my throat when I looked up into the worried eyes of Taylor Vaughn. Kane was behind him, but he was on the phone with someone. My cousin glanced my way, then back over to Taylor, watching him as he walked toward me.

"Are you okay?" Taylor asked, moving in close to stand in front of me. When he took one of my hands, I closed my eyes from the warmth of his fingers, but quickly pulled away, dropping it as if his hand had burned me.

"I have a small concussion," I said, honestly. "Doc wants me to be watched over the next twenty-four hours or so."

"You will be staying on the bus with us," Kane told me, pulling a chair over to the side of the bed. He turned it around so that he could straddle it and fold his arms across the back of the chair. He rested his chin on his arms and let out a harsh breath, "They haven't found him."

"Well, that's just great," I said angrily, throwing my hands in the air. "I really hope the fucker comes back."

"*No*," both men barked, causing my body to jerk back from the venom dripping off of their outburst. If looks could kill, the two men in front of me would've been arrested for murder.

"I won't be caught off guard again," I vowed.

"Because someone will be with you until we leave in the morning," Taylor said, nudging me over so that he could sit next to me on the bed. I glanced at Kane, who wasn't showing any protectiveness at Taylor invading my personal space. Maybe I did hit my head really hard and I was actually hallucinating?

"And someone will be around you for the rest of the tour," Kane announced.

"We really need to go," I hurried them along, ignoring Kane's statement. "You guys need to get back."

"The meet and greet can take place without us," Kane said, rolling his hazel eyes. God, we looked so much alike when he did that.

"Do you know if I can go now?" I asked, looking around Kane to the door.

As if summoned, the nurse knocked quietly and pushed through the door. Her eyes landed on Taylor and no one could've missed the way she pushed her big breasts up higher as if she were offering them to an ancient god for a sacrifice.

"Ms. Maddox," she greeted, once she noticed I had stood up from the bed. I had to do something with my hands or I would've punched the bitch harder than I'd done to Doug the other day.

"Yes?" I replied, not even looking at her as I grabbed Taylor's coat he'd put over me when he'd found me laying on the cold hard ground.

"Here are your discharge papers," she smiled, holding the papers out toward me, but her eyes were on Taylor. If she could've laid herself out on the bed and offered herself up for the taking, then I'm sure she would've done it with no second thought.

"Hey, nurse Nancy…*I'm* the patient. So, talk to me, would ya?" I interrupted, moving between her and Taylor. I heard him chuckle behind me, and I glanced over at my cousin who was now standing by the door looking like he was about to explode from the built up need to laugh his ass off.

"Um," she blushed, knowing I'd caught her looking at the sexy guitarist. I didn't blame her for flirting. Oh…well, who the hell was I kidding? I wanted to claw her eyes out so she'd never look at him again.

"Just give me the damn papers," I groused, snatching them from her hand. I signed them quickly, shoving the forms back at her. "Can I go?"

"Oh…um, yeah," she cleared her throat. "Yes…yes, you can leave."

"Good," I snarled, pushing past her as I made my way out of the room.

Eric was waiting by the exit with the SUV to take us back to the venue when I exited the glass doors to the emergency room. I didn't say anything as I climbed in the backseat and sat between Kane and Taylor. I leaned my head on the back of the seat and closed my eyes.

Soft hands stroked my cheek and I burrowed down into the warmth that held me in its safe grasp. "*Cora.*"

God, that voice. Those hands, although rough, were warm yet tender. It felt as if I were in a cocoon where nothing could harm me. For a moment, I slipped deeper into the sleep my body had needed for the past four months that I'd been on the road. It was heaven.

"Baby girl, wake up," Taylor whispered, still holding my face.

I blinked a few times before his handsome face came into view. Why the hell did he have to be so gorgeous? He was an Adonis, perfectly made…chiseled from a one-of-a-kind stone that was priceless.

"Sorry," I said, closing my eyes for a split second, trying to absorb his touch one last time before we had to go back to the real world. "I'm so tired." That statement held two different meanings. I was tired physically. I was also tired of fighting him. I felt tears prick my eyes. All I wanted to do was to let them fall and beg Taylor to take over for me…just until I felt better.

"I know you are, Cora," he said softly, reaching over to unbuckle my seatbelt. I hadn't realized that I'd leaned over in my sleep and had used him for a pillow…a bed. "Come on, let me get you to the bunk."

"No," I moaned. "Work…"

"You are off for the night," he informed me, opening the door. "You are going onto the bus with us and staying where Kane and I can watch you. Rita is taking care of everything else."

"Is it okay not to argue with you?" I asked, feeling groggy.

Taylor chuckled and held out his hand to help me from the vehicle. I was too damn tired to argue with him about anything at the moment.

"I really wish you'd let me take care of you for once, Coraline," he whispered. In fact, I was so groggy, I wasn't sure I had heard him right. I smiled to myself when I tossed those words around in my head. I'd never given up my control to anyone, but a part of me wanted to just let go...just let him take some of that control away from me.

I opened my eyes and realized that he was still there, our noses so close they almost touched. He was worried. I could tell from the little crease in the corner of his right eye. His soft lips were pressed into a hard line that assured me that he was very stressed at what had happened to me.

I sighed heavily, climbing out of the SUV. When my feet hit the ground, I wanted to collapse from exhaustion. It was a task to put one foot in front of the other. Thankfully, Taylor picked me up and held me tight to his chest as he walked toward the bus. I rested my head on his shoulder and let him take care of me. For once, I gave over the reins of my control, letting someone else call the shots.

I liked it way more than I should. I had always been in control of everything around me. The fact that I gave that up to him now? That was saying a lot about how I was faring at the moment. The fact that I liked it…scared the fucking shit out of me.

CHAPTER 8

Taylor

She fit against my chest like one half of a custom made puzzle that only consisted of two pieces to complete the set. I was almost a foot taller than her, but somehow we worked. Coraline's tiny frame was curved in all the right places and soft...oh, God was she soft. My cock twitched in my jeans when I remembered running my hands up and down her naked body when we'd been alone on that island. Well, *fuck*! I needed to quit thinking about her naked. I had to get her inside the bus and safely into a bunk so we could keep an eye on her.

I didn't want to wake her up, but we'd arrived at the venue. Kane and Eric slipped out of the backseat after I told Kane to go inside and make his appearance. I wasn't part of the band, so I could afford to miss a meet and greet from time to time. Tonight was pretty stressful for both of us. Seeing Coraline unconscious on the floor with a battered face scared a few years off both mine and Kane's lives.

As I walked onto the bus with her in my arms, I smiled at the note Ash had left on the table.

Take Cora to the back bedroom. You can stay in there with her.

Shit…Did everyone know we had something going on?

I shook the questions from my mind and moved forward, passing the bunk where I slept. The bedroom door was ajar and the sheets on the queen size bed were already pulled back. In true rockstar fashion, the black sheets and black comforter were designed for a sexual romp even though all of the band members of *Glory Days* were already married and didn't play around with the ladies anymore.

"Taylor," Coraline moaned, squinting her eyes.

"What's wrong, baby?" I whispered, knowing that her head was probably killing her. "Are you hurting?"

"Yes," she said, swallowing. "Thirsty."

"I'll get you something," I said, laying her out on the bed. The loss of her touch left a sharp pain in my chest, but knowing that I was taking on the responsibility of her care made it ease a bit. I found the prescription pain killers the doc had prescribed and a bottled water, hurrying back to her side.

"Here," I said, sliding my arm behind her shoulders to help her sit up.

"Thank you," she said, taking the pill and water from my other hand.

"We want you to rest and stay with us for the next few days," I said, not liking that I said "we" when all I wanted to do was say, "I want you to stay with me."

"I just want to sleep for two days," she mumbled. "Then I'll be good as new."

"I'm sure you will," I chuckled, seeing the Coraline I'd fallen for all those months ago. "I'll wake you in a few hours to check on you."

Just as she drifted off to sleep, I heard soft footsteps climb the bus stairs. Looking through the door that I'd left open, I saw a flash of pink hair and knew Rita had come to sit with her while I was onstage.

"Hey," she whispered. "How is she?"

"She's hurting," I admitted, standing up from the bed. "She just took a pain pill and should be out of it for a few hours." I turned and pulled the covers over her to keep her warm. She looked so soft and beautiful in her sleep. It was all I could do not to climb in the bed with her and hold her until she was better.

"I'll take care of her, Taylor," Rita comforted, placing a reassuring hand on my shoulder.

"Okay," I nodded. "I'll be back after the show."

The concert seemed to last forever. We'd performed and blew the crowd away. I was thankful for the opportunity to be onstage with these guys. My band was not quite as big as *Glory Days*, but *Fatal Cross* was holding their own since our comeback two years ago. It was amazing the things you could accomplish when you were clean and sober.

The crew rushed around us, taking down the equipment so we could hurry on to the next stop. I, on the other hand, was in a hurry to lay eyes on Cora. I just wanted to make sure she was okay. After a quick shower in the arena, I hurried over to the bus where I found Kane cursing for all he was worth.

"That stubborn little shit should not be working," he bellowed, throwing his hands in the air.

"Cora?" I asked, looking at the guys who were standing around a very scared looking

Rita. Her pink hair was in disarray and she looked worried.

"She snuck off the bus and apparently thought it was okay to go back to work," Ash sighed. "Someone needs to go inside and kick her ass."

"I'll do it," I mumbled. No one said anything as I hurried down the steps of the bus.

Kane did stick his head out of the doors as I was halfway across the lot and yelled, "Make her get her ass back to bed!"

"I will," I called out, giving her cousin a thumbs up as I reached the doors.

Flinging them open, I dodged a few roadies who were wheeling cases toward the double doors. I scanned the backstage area looking for that fucker, Doug. I still hadn't heard if he'd been caught, and no one had said anything about him contacting any of his friends on the crew. As far as I was concerned, the faster we got out of this city...the better for everyone. I hoped the jackass had to hitchhike back to whatever rock he crawled out from underneath of.

"What the fuck are you doing?" I yelled, looking up into the scaffolding she was climbing. "Get your ass down from there right now!"

"No," she huffed, swaying a little as she took the next step. My heart raced in my chest and I felt myself fill with panic at the idea of her falling to her death.

She wasn't going to just come down because I demanded it. No, Coraline Maddox didn't do anything she was told. That woman had to do things her own way. I'm sure when she finally meets St. Peter at the pearly gates, she'll probably argue with him as to when *she* was ready to walk through to spend her eternity. Hell, knowing her, she'd argue with the devil himself if she didn't like the way things were run in hell, too.

It took about ten minutes before she sighed heavily and made her way down the ladder. I stood with my arms folded across my chest and watched as the little pixie gathered up a handful of wires, coiling them in a perfect loop before putting them away in a tote.

"You need to be in bed," I said, stopping in front of her so that she couldn't pass.

"I have to work, Taylor," she pouted, averting her eyes. "I'm actually feeling much better."

"Liar," I growled, seeing that she had zero color to her usually rosy cheeks. She was as pale as a ghost. Her eyes looked weary and extremely exhausted.

"Now he's interested in my health," she grumbled under her breath. For a moment, I thought she'd said something different, but I quickly realized she was talking about her anger at me not calling.

"Coraline," I whispered. "I'm sorry…for not calling you. Were you sick?"

"Leave it…leave it alone," she bit out through gritted teeth. I saw the moisture well up in the corners of her eyes. I wanted to punch myself for putting that amount of pain in her beautiful eyes, but I was done with her avoiding my questions.

"No," I said, reaching for her arm as she passed. "We need to talk about this."

"No, we don't," she snapped, jerking her arm away from me. "It's over, Taylor. *We* are over. It should've never happened, and it sure as hell won't happen again." She moved around me at a fast pace. It was like watching the Energizer bunny running circles around where I stood. The woman didn't stop moving unless she was asleep. I picked up a black cord that was taped to the ground and swung it around playfully in my hand.

"Damn it, Coraline," I snarled, stopping her from ignoring me by walking away. She'd finally gotten close enough for me to touch, again. "I'm going to hogtie you to this fucking microphone stand if you don't stop what the fuck you are doing and talk to me."

"You wouldn't," she pushed, placing a hand on her hip.

"Try me, sweet cheeks," I growled, still twirling the cord around in my hand. "And don't even think about running, because I will catch you."

"Go to hell, Taylor," she growled back, turning her shoulder and brushing her way past me.

I made a split second decision to reach out with one hand and grab her upper arm where it wasn't bruised. With the other hand, I snatched the microphone stand, pulling it over in front of where I'd stopped her in her tracks. With quick accuracy that even I was shocked at, I twined the cord around her wrists, binding her to the stand within seconds.

"What the hell are you doing?" she cursed, glaring daggers at me. Damn, I really wanted to kiss that smart ass mouth into submission.

"You have been avoiding me and I want answers," I demanded. "Woman! You are driving me crazy!"

"*I'm* driving *you* crazy?" she roared. I placed my heavy boot on the bottom of the mic stand, locking her in place. I watched as she wiggled her fingers, looking for any give in my bindings. She found none. "Untie me!"

"No," I barked angrily, standing my ground. "Not until you tell me why you hate me so badly."

"I...I don't hate you, Taylor," she confessed, defeated. I noticed how her shoulders dropped from exhaustion, but I didn't move forward to hold on to her, even though my every instinct was to pick her up and carry her to a soft bed so she could rest from her injuries.

"Then there's something you are not telling me," I scolded, throwing my hands in the air. "You are mad at me for something I don't even know I did, Coraline. Do you know how frustrating that is? I can't even make things better with you because you won't tell me what I did wrong!"

"Was your phone broken? For a month?" She cursed and yanked on her bindings, still not able to slip free. I saw the first tear drop from her eye before she leaned forward, wiping her face on the shoulder of her cotton shirt.

"I…I was, damn," I responded, skirting the truth. "I was away."

"Where, Taylor?" she demanded, the life flared back into her beautiful eyes. She was angry. Angry was so much better than mopey and depressed. "Away, where? Were you off doing drugs? I thought you were clean."

"I *am* clean," I scowled. "I haven't touched anything in over two years."

"Is...is there someone else?" she questioned softly. I saw the sadness in her eyes and knew that standing on stage wasn't where we needed to be holding this conversation.

"We need to find somewhere more private," I mumbled, unwrapping her hands from the mic stand. I took both of them into my hands and rubbed the feeling back into her wrists and fingers, mindful of her injuries. She moaned gently at my touch and I smiled warmly, because I felt the same way when her tiny hands touched me.

I pulled her along, not dropping the hold I had on her hand. Coraline would run away given the chance, and I was tired of her bolting instead of talking to me. We were about to get to the bottom of this and hopefully move forward. That was, if Coraline Maddox could forgive me for being an idiot.

CHAPTER 9

Taylor

I found a backroom where we could have some privacy. The switch on the wall beside the door clicked when I flipped on the lights, pulling her inside the room. I slammed the door shut and threw the lock before turning around to see her glaring at my chest. She wouldn't even look me in the eyes as she folded her arms across her chest.

I stood in front of the door with my arms crossed over my chest, ensuring she couldn't slip out without moving my body out of the way and fumbling with the lock. We needed to finally talk about this thing...whatever it was between us.

"There hasn't been anyone else since you," I admitted, pulling her close to my chest. I kissed the top of her head sweetly, inhaling her natural scent. She felt so right in my arms.

"I...I can't do this," she squeaked out, but betrayed herself by clenching my shirt tightly in her fists. I felt her shoulders start to shake, and I tried to push her back so that I could look into her beautiful hazel eyes, but she held on for dear life and buried her face in my chest.

"What happened, Cora?" I asked, stroking her short hair, stopping so that I could cup the side of her face. Being careful of her bruises, I tilted her head back, feeling my heart crack from the torture in her beautiful face. This had nothing to do with the attack that'd happened as a result of a roadie with a death wish.

Whatever was going on with Cora, I wanted to fix it. Seeing her hurt and shaken up over something that I may or may not have done had totally thrown me out of my element. I wanted to kill whoever had hurt her or fix whatever was broken. My heart physically ached seeing her so upset, because I knew that I was the reason she was upset. I'd done this to her, and I hated myself for it.

"Baby, you have to talk to me," I urged, seeing as she wasn't talking through the tears streaming down her face. "I can't make things better if I don't know what the hell is going on with you." She didn't look like Cora in that moment. This headstrong woman, who was in charge of every aspect of her life, stood before me with her eyes downcast and her body slumped almost in defeat.

"Taylor...," she swallowed. "I...I..."

"What is it?" I begged, my voice cracking as I spoke.

"Why didn't you call me?" she asked, her voice only a whisper. She'd cast her gaze to the floor again after a quick glance at my face, and I wasn't sure if she was hiding from me or from my answer. It felt like she didn't want to see me shut her down in person.

"I was going to call you, but we'd been busy at the studio," I sighed, very heavily. "I had a bad week after that…things were stressful, and I just wanted to get high. My dealer showed up at my house and offered me some coke. It took all I had to tell him I wasn't interested, and after that, I called my sponsor. I ended up staying with him for a few weeks. By that time, I thought I could just wait another few weeks to see you and then explain in person."

"So you didn't do any drugs?" she asked, biting her lower lip. At that moment, all I wanted to do was to pull her lip away and bite it as I kissed her. The urge to comfort her was a driving need inside me.

"No, baby girl," I smiled, brushing my thumb over her bottom lip and pulling it away from her teeth. "I didn't."

"Thank God," she breathed. Her shoulders relaxed with my words, and I vowed right then and there that I would never do anything again to make this tiny woman doubt my words. I didn't need illegal drugs anymore…I needed Coraline Maddox, because I was quickly becoming addicted to her. "I'm so proud of you."

"What did you want to talk to me about?" I asked. It was her turn to finally tell me why she'd blown up my phone for a few days before I'd gone MIA.

"It was nothing really," she said, looking away sadly.

"Yes, it was something, Coraline," I said, pulling her back to my chest when she started to pull away. "It was obviously something, because you haven't given me the time of day since I stepped foot on this tour and your cousin glares daggers at me every time we are in the same room."

"He does?" she scowled, narrowing her eyes. The little pixie made me smile with her harsh stare. She was so tiny and completely petite that no one would take her anger seriously. That's why her mouth always got her into trouble. The fact that she was so upset honestly worried me. She wasn't acting like herself.

Her phone rang, stopping our conversation. I started to protest and take her phone away, but she raised her hand, halting my action. "It's Eric. This could be important."

She answered the phone and pushed away from me while she listened to what the band's head of security had to say. It seems that Doug was still on the loose. Her face flushed in anger at whatever Eric was saying.

My protective side flared and all I wanted to do was to hide her under my skin, shielding her from any danger. Cora wouldn't allow that, because she was too strong a woman to have a man fight her battles for her. I just wished she'd let me care for her the way I longed to do.

"I have to go talk to the police again," she complained.

"Do you need me to go with you?" I volunteered, reaching out to take her tiny hand into my own. The connection between us when we touched could light the world on fire, if she'd just let me inside that hardened shell of her's. I stroked my thumb over the back of her hand, trying to calm not only her nerves, but my own.

"No," she said, shaking her head. I watched as her eyes dropped to our joined hands. I felt the tension release from her muscles, but only for a moment. Her hand jerked as if I'd burned her, causing me to frown when she jerked her hand away completely. "I need to do this on my own."

"Okay, but I'm here," I promised. She nodded her understanding and headed for the door.

Watching her walk away, I made a vow. Before we finished the show in Los Angeles, I would know exactly why she wouldn't talk to me or even come clean about why she was so angry when I didn't answer her calls after we'd been back from the island.

I had a bad feeling whatever Cora had to tell me was going to turn my world upside down.

CHAPTER 10

Taylor

She closed up and wouldn't talk to me. Cora spent the next few hours avoiding any type of contact, and that was just starting to piss me off. Every time I felt like I was getting close to breaking that shell around the hardened woman, she would clam up again and leave me in the dust as she ran away from whatever demons she was harboring.

It was time to head out to our last stop on the tour. The guys had all finished their calls home and we settled down in the living area of the bus to unwind for the night. The bus jerked as we headed out of the parking lot.

"How's Cora?" Kane asked as he slid into the half-circled booth seat behind the table.

"She's Cora," I said, dropping my head into my hands. "She's driving me crazy. I don't know what the hell she is keeping from me, but whatever it is, she's stressed and I'm stressed. It's killing both of us."

"She hasn't talked to you?" Kane asked, his voice sounding surprised. He'd just sat down from throwing his beer can in the trash and changing into a ripped up concert shirt that looked like it'd seen better days.

"No," I responded, looking up into his eyes. "I'm sorry, Kane, but I really don't want to talk to you about my relationship with your cousin." There was no way in *hell* I was going down that road with nowhere to run and hide. I was bigger than her cousin, but I wouldn't cross that man, even on my best day.

"I think maybe you damn well should," he urged, teeth gritting in anger. I raised a brow, wondering what the hell was eating at him. Something wasn't right. I could *feel* it.

"Kane," Ash warned, standing up to get between the two of us. I frowned at the lead singer, completely oblivious as to what the hell was going on.

"No," he barked, stepping around Ash. Ash placed a hand on Kane's shoulders, stopping him from moving any closer. I stood up, bracing myself for whatever this guy was going to say or do. "This has gone on too damn long. I stayed out of it, because she begged me to keep my mouth shut. I'm done playing the nice guy."

"What the hell are you talking about?" I demanded, my own anger boiling to the surface. "I'm so sick and fucking tired of these half-assed answers from her…you glaring at me like you are about to kill me at any moment. God dammit! What the *fuck* is going on!? I want answers and I want them right now!" I was so done with this whole situation. If Coraline wasn't worth fighting for, then I'd have the driver pull off at the next town and I'd fly my ass home.

"Both of you calm the hell down," Ash reprimanded, playing the peacemaker. "Kane...chill the fuck out for a moment and back off." Kane took a deep breath and stepped back, but his body didn't relax.

"Taylor," Ash addressed me, getting my attention. "This needs to be handled delicately. Do you two think you can talk this out without going to blows?"

"*I'm* the one who's been left in the dark here for about three months too long," I bitched, running my hand through my hair. "Kane is the one who is acting like he wants to pound my face into the ground. I could understand that if I knew *what the fuck I did wrong!*"

"You two need to talk," Reed interrupted, standing up from his seat and slapping Kane on the shoulder. "Go. Talk to him, man." The room grew quiet as Kane and I both calmed down. My heart still raced, because whatever he had to tell me was going to be big. It didn't take a rocket scientist to realize that bad news was coming.

"Come on," Kane said, jutting his chin out toward the back of the bus where Coraline should've been resting but was too busy working with a slight concussion. "Let's head back to the bedroom to talk."

Ash and Reed sat heavily at the table, both of them with grim expressions on their faces. My heart continued to pound in my chest, sweat beaded up on my palms, and I squared my shoulders, knowing that whatever Kane had to say was going to break me.

I sat heavily on the bed in the back room of the bus as Kane shut the door and leaned back against it. He crossed his arms across his chest and pinched the bridge of his nose in frustration. "She hasn't said anything to you? Nothing at all?"

"No," I barked, jumping to my feet. "What the fuck is going on, Kane? I've had it with this bullshit. What the fuck is Coraline hiding from me?" My temper was at a fevered pitch. My hands clenched at my sides, because I had the sudden urge to punch something. My mind was all over the grid with the possibilities of what had happened, but until someone told me, I was stuck only getting half answers. Those half answers were really starting to piss me the hell off.

"Coraline called me two months ago," he began, the flash of pain in his eyes caused my heart to increase in speed…something wasn't right…something was terribly wrong. "It was two in the morning and she said she needed to go the hospital. Delilah and I rushed out to her place, and what I found there scared ten years off my life."

"What the hell is wrong with her?" I demanded, my heart stopped beating for a moment. Was she sick?

"She was bleeding," he sighed. I felt all of the blood drain from my face. My brain spun and I swear I saw stars dance across my vision. The feeling was strange. It was like my brain knew what was coming and was preparing itself for a fatal blow. A blow that would definitely change my life.

"Bleeding?" I gasped, my mind churning over a million reasons why she would be bleeding. Did she fall? Cut herself? I don't remember seeing any scars and she wasn't in any type of bandaging or brace.

"Taylor, she was pregnant," Kane admitted. My ears rang, causing me to automatically shake my head to restore all of the blood that had just drained from there to my shattered heart. I reached out, grabbing ahold of his forearm to keep me steady, because at any moment, I thought I was going to go down into a large heap on the floor.

"What?" I breathed, my heart falling into the pit of my stomach. "Wait! You said 'was'? Oh, God!" The words were there in my head, but they wouldn't register. Bleeding...He said *was bleeding*.

"She was having a miscarriage," Kane confirmed, his eyes glistened with the beginning of tears that didn't fall. "She lost the baby." I heard the desperation and sadness in his voice. His baby cousin had been pregnant and I was the low down, dirty asshole who didn't come running to her side when she needed me the most. No wonder he acted like he wanted me dead...I'd never forgive myself for that either.

"No," I cried, dropping to my knees. I buried my head into my hands and wept. I'd ignored her calls. I'd left her alone to deal with this and I did *nothing*! "This is my fault."

"No," Kane quickly responded, placing a reassuring hand on my shoulder. "It wasn't your fault, man. The doctors said that the baby wasn't viable. It was nothing that she could've prevented."

The baby wasn't viable? Our little baby wasn't strong enough?

Oh, God. Cora!

No!

No!

"I didn't answer the phone," I whimpered, speaking to myself, but also aloud. "I never called her back. I...I was too damn concerned about myself. What have I done?"

My Coraline, my girl...she'd had been alone...probably scared. What type of man...*human being* was I that I let her go through that alone? I'd never be able to make it right.

"What *were* you doing during that time?" Kane inquired. When I looked into my friend's eyes, I saw concern, anger, betrayal, and...understanding.

"I was having a hard time, Kane," I admitted, looking at him with pleading eyes.

"With the new album, I was on edge. You know how it is. The stress got to me and then my dealer showed up at the house. I sent him away and called my sponsor. I packed a bag and headed to his place for a bit. I needed some time to clear my head. Cora had been calling, but I was too fucking busy for her. By the time I'd gotten my shit together, the phone calls had stopped. I figured I could apologize in person."

"You *are* still clean, right?" he asked.

"Yes, hell yes I am," I informed him, moving to sit down on the bed. I couldn't trust my legs to stand on their own anymore.

"You need to talk to her," Kane told me, sighing heavily.

"You and I both know that Coraline Maddox has a mind of her own," I stressed. "She'll run from me."

"Then you have to strong arm her," he growled. "*Make* her talk to you, Taylor. She will try to run. If you care about her as much as I think you do, then you'll find a way to make this right. It's killing both of you and I'm tired of seeing pain in her eyes...and yours."

"I'll talk to her," I promised. "She won't be alone again."

Kane nodded and left me alone in the back bedroom. I covered my eyes with my hands and let the moisture fall, not caring to wipe it away. I'd had a bad feeling that whatever she was hiding from me was huge, but I had no idea it was this big. I had no idea that I was the father of a child that never even had a chance to live.

At some point in my grief, I must've fallen asleep. It was only then that I remembered the night on the island and the dream was so vivid, it was like I was there all over again.

I slid on my shades to cover my eyes from the bright afternoon sunlight. The ocean breeze blew across my face, causing the scent of coconut oil to register in my brain. My eyes scanned the area as I walked toward the water, a towel slung over my shoulder.

I'd come to this island for one purpose, and one purpose only…to find Coraline Maddox. I knew she'd frequented this place in the Azores when she wasn't touring with her cousin's band. She'd talked about this place with a dreamy expression on her face and swore that she was going to make this trip an annual one because of how much she loved taking a break at this little resort.

Now, my crazy ass self was stalking the poor woman halfway around the world, just so that I could possibly get to know her a little better. Yeah, we'd flirted on the tour the previous year, but she'd never given me the time of day.

Well, that was a lie. There'd been one night, a night that I remember well, where we'd bumped into each other as I was exiting the green room at the venue in Salt Lake City and she'd been rushing through to find one of the band members. My hands had automatically latched onto her thick hips, *steadying her as she gasped in shock when she realized there was someone standing in the doorway. After her head snapped up from the clipboard she'd been holding, I saw her beautiful hazel eyes darken seductively.*

"Oh, I'm sorry, Taylor," she breathed. We'd been so close, our lips were only inches apart. It'd taken every ounce of willpower I had to keep from claiming her lush mouth right then and there.

"Slow down, baby girl," I teased, but the smile I gave her was nothing close to humorous. No, it was predatory and she knew it. My eyes latched onto her lips and I felt my cock harden when her tiny, pink tongue snaked out to moisten her bottom lip. If it wasn't for her mic crackling to life with someone calling for her to help with something on stage, I would've stolen a kiss from her then.

Now, here I was, standing on a beach, hovering over a sexy woman who was laid out on a chair, soaking up the sun in a navy blue string bikini. It was more string than bikini, and her ample breasts, flat stomach, and silky legs were shining with the lotion she'd applied before laying back.

"Are you going to stand in my sun all day or introduce...Oh!" she admonished, stopping when she opened her eyes and noticed who was invading her space.

"Cora," I purred possessively. Holy fuck, she looked hot enough to eat. I took a moment and glanced around to see if there were any men, and when I noticed three off to her left staring at her like dogs in heat, I raised my glasses and narrowed my eyes, silently telling them to turn the fuck around. I was about to stake my claim on Coraline Maddox, and consequences be dammed.

"Taylor," she stammered, looking surprised. "What are you doing here?"

"I'm on vacation," I casually shrugged. "What are you doing here?"

"I'm on vacation too," she smiled, but it didn't reach her eyes.

"Mind if I take a chair next to yours?" I asked, really not caring if she denied me or not. I was going to be close to her for the next three days if it killed me. I didn't even wait for her to answer before I tossed my towel on the chair. Removing my shirt, I noticed when Cora's head cocked slightly to the left, hiding her stare behind those dark sunglasses she wore.

"Uh, sure," she whispered, but not low enough that I missed the desire in her voice.

"Want to go for a swim with me?" I flirted, holding out my hand. When her tiny fingers slipped into my palm, I felt like I could move mountains with the happiness surging inside me.

"Sure," she nodded, rising to her feet when I gave her a little tug.

We spent the next three hours lounging and swimming. By the time the sun had started its downward trek, I found that I wasn't quite ready to leave her side.

"Have dinner with me?" I blurted. She'd started gathering her things, placing them into a striped bag that was stored underneath the chair she'd claimed as her own for the day.

"I don't know, Taylor," she hesitated, crinkling her nose. "I don't like mixing work and my private life."

"Have we even talked about work today?" I asked. I had a point to get across to this woman, and I wasn't going to take no for an answer.

"Well, no," she admitted, shaking her head slightly. The short black locks of hair slicked toward the back, showing off her beautiful eyes when the sun touched them just right. I found my hands itching to tighten into the back of her head to see if I could get a palm full of her hair while I kissed her senseless. "No, we haven't."

"So, you are not mixing anything with anything," I stated. "Simple as that. So…dinner, yeah?"

I watched as several emotions played across her face. She wanted to have dinner with me, but was afraid. Her body language betrayed her indecision by *leaning toward me, her hands wringing in nervousness. I didn't even give her a chance to tell me to take a hike.*

"Go take a shower, get dressed, and meet me downstairs in one hour for dinner," I ordered, before standing up and walking away. I'd only made it a few steps before I turned around and caught her gaping at my back. "Don't keep me waiting, Coraline."

It was an hour on the dot when I turned from my seat at the bar to find Coraline standing at the entrance to the restaurant wearing a simple sundress that had no straps over the shoulders, just some material that kept it tight across her large breasts. I had to grab ahold of the bar to keep from falling on my face when all of the blood in my brain raced to my cock so that it could be ready to take this woman back to my room.

Oh, who the hell was I kidding? Coraline Maddox wouldn't let me boss her around unless she approved of it first. She wasn't that type of woman. No, she was the definition of a bad ass bitch.

"You look stunning," I said, kissing her cheek as we greeted.

"Thank you," she blushed. The slight dusting of pink across her cheeks almost did me in, but I gritted my teeth and followed the hostess to our table.

We ate dinner and laughed over a few bottles of wine, and before I knew what had happened, we were in her room, tearing each other's clothes off.

I blinked and everything went dark. Coraline was somewhere off in the distance, causing me to jump from the bed in search of her frantic cries. My feet slipped out from underneath me when I stepped in something warm and wet, sending my body across the floor. Flashes of light to my left showed glimpses of my girl huddled in a corner…blood covering her body and the floor upon which I laid, unable to reach her when she needed me the most.

My eyes popped open as I gasped out in fright. I brushed my hand down my face, willing my heart to slow down from the nightmare that woke me. My mind was processing what I'd been told the night before, but I knew that the nightmare I'd just experienced was nothing compared to what was going to happen as soon as I confronted her with the fact that I now knew why she'd called.

I had no idea how to make Cora understand how sorry I was for being a complete asshole and letting her suffer alone. I'd spend the rest of my life making it up to her if that's what I had to do to make her happy again.

CHAPTER 11

Coraline

Every step I took, my face throbbed and the knot on the side of my head ached. The police had questioned me about Doug and I was also told that I should get a restraining order. Eric, the band's head of security, said he'd take care of it as soon as possible. Doug was still on the run and I seriously doubted the jerk would come looking for me. He was probably laying low under a rock somewhere in the desert. There was so much weed found in the room that he'd be put away for a long time as soon as he was located.

There was only one more show, and that was the hometown return in Los Angeles. After the six shows overseas, I was off for the next year. I'd already made plans on a lengthy vacation somewhere private...and away from

Taylor Vaughn. I needed a break. Why the hell did that thought hurt my chest?

I couldn't spend any more time with him. Having him around over the past couple of weeks was nice, but also a test to my mental health. Every time he walked by, I would catch his masculine scent, and that sent my brain into a death spiral, remembering the time we'd had on the island. Then I'd remember the night Kane and Delilah rushed me to the emergency room. I couldn't keep this up. I had to get over him before it killed me.

The band's bus had already departed after I'd refused to spend any more time in the bed. Taylor had put up a fuss, but I silenced him with a hard glare. Kane wasn't too happy about me not being under his watchful eye, either. Thankfully, they didn't argue about me riding with the other crew. It didn't take long to understand why they'd given in so easily.

"The boys asked me to keep an eye on you," Rita admitted, rolling her eyes at what she had to say. "I told them I would. So, please don't get me fired by passing out and hitting your noggin or anything." We both laughed loudly as I pushed her toward the leather couch.

"Your loyalty to me is golden, my friend," I grinned, bumping shoulders with her.

"Anytime, chica," she winked. "So, when are you going to finally give in and jump Taylor's bones?"

"Ugh," I groaned. "Please don't even start."

"The puppy dog eyes from *both* of you are getting old," she teased.

"I...I don't know what you're talking about, Rita," I lied, but she wasn't fooled.

"Coraline Maddox...you are a fool if you don't see that man watching your every move," she sighed, shaking her head. "When he found you unconscious...he was pale as a ghost. He would've given you his heart if you'd needed it.

I don't know what history the two of you have or what the big deal is that you won't give him a chance, but that man is head over heels in love with you, Cora."

"It's complicated," I grumbled, lowering my voice so that none of the other crew could hear us talking. "And he is *not* in love with me."

"Well, you need to uncomplicated things," she scolded. "I think that man would lay the world at your feet if you'd get over whatever it is that is keeping you two at odds."

I didn't reply, but I did nod my understanding and bit my lower lip in concern. Rita was right, and I'd clouded my mind with my anger at him for not answering when I needed him the most. Yes, it still hurt my heart something fierce. I needed to tell him, but he was already gone. I ignored everyone and found my way to my bunk, falling asleep as soon as my head hit the pillow.

When I opened my eyes again, I heard whispered voices out in the living area of the huge bus. I rolled over and pulled a pillow over my head to drown out the noise. It didn't take long before I felt myself drifting off to sleep.

"Cora," Taylor cooed, touching the side of my face, softly. I knew it was him attempting to wake me, but I was too comfortable to respond. I heard him chuckle when I groaned in my sleep and tried to bat his hands away.

"Sleep," I pouted, hoping he'd leave me alone.

"Come on, sleepyhead," he chuckled, taking a seat beside me on the mattress. "You need to wake up...I need to talk to you."

"No...talking," I moaned.

"I brought coffee," he announced, causing me to open one eye to verify that he brought the drink of the gods to my bedside. "Before you ask, yes...there is vanilla and a bucket load of sugar in there. Do you know that you will probably have diabetes in the next year if you keep drinking your coffee this way?"

"It's the way I like it," I argued, throwing the covers aside. When I opened my eyes fully, Taylor's green gaze had darkened and his nostrils were flared as he took in my body. I didn't even try to cover myself. I wore dark purple boy shorts and two tanks tops, doubled for support. At least they weren't white where my nipples could be seen. These were both black. Obviously, he liked what he saw, because I noticed he shifted his hips into a more comfortable position.

"You look beautiful," he declared, holding out his free hand to help me from the bottom bunk. I averted my eyes when I noticed his obvious erection pressing against the front of his dark denim jeans.

"Thank you for the coffee," I responded, walking toward the front of the bus. "Hey, where is everyone?"

"They all headed inside for a bit," he began, taking a seat at the small kitchen table by the window. "We should talk."

"Oh," I grimaced, taking a seat next to him in the bench seat. "I'm really over what I was mad about, Taylor. Let's just go on and forget it happened." His eyes fell dark, and I had a feeling I knew why he'd come.

"No, Coraline," he said sadly, his voice deepened. As I turned toward him, I was shocked at the moisture welling up in his eyes. "I want to know why you didn't tell me that you were pregnant with my child."

CHAPTER 12

Taylor

"Because you wouldn't answer your fucking phone!" Coraline exploded, throwing the mug of coffee in my face. Thankfully, it was already cooled enough to not scald my shoulder where it landed when I turned my head.

"I'm so sorry, Cora," I apologized, moving toward her after she bolted from the seat. "I was a selfish asshole, baby. I would've been there for you."

"But you weren't, Taylor," she cried, the tears pouring from her eyes now. She crossed her arms over her ample breasts and paced in front of the couch on the bus. I tried to reach for her, but she jerked her arm out of my reach. "Don't! Don't touch me! I…I can't think when you touch me."

"No," I hollered, stopping her from moving away from me by standing in front of her and crossing my arms to keep her from darting around me to run off the bus. It was my turn to get angry. "You don't get to block me out, Coraline. I want to know…I deserve to know. Why didn't you tell me as soon as I got here? Why did you keep avoiding me?"

"I…I tried to call you several times," she bawled, lowering her crossed arms to cover her now empty stomach. I wanted to reach out for her and pull her into the safety of my arms. I didn't want her to suffer any more than she already had, but this suffering I couldn't protect her from. This was something that I'd done, and I had no idea how to make the agony go away. "You never answered and I figured you were done with me…that you'd only thought of what we did as a one night stand."

"It wasn't," I whispered, fighting back my own tears at seeing her so upset. It killed me to see her in pain.

"How was I to know?" she yelled. "I felt like the dirtiest of whores, Taylor! Then I wake up, two weeks after I found out I was pregnant...and..." That was when she collapsed to her knees and I followed her movements, taking her into my arms.

"I'm so sorry, baby," I chanted repeatedly into her short hair. "I should've answered the phone. There will never be enough apologies in my life to tell you how sorry I am for what I did, Coraline."

"I don't even know if it was a boy or a girl," she confessed, scrambling up so that she was sitting in my lap on the floor of the bus. I didn't really care where we were, she could find her comfort in my lap anywhere she wanted. Right now, she kept her still battered face pressed into my chest as she cried.

"It was too soon, I'm sure," I added, hoping I was right. "How...How far along were you?"

"Six…weeks," she said, taking a deep breath. "I wasn't even pregnant long enough to get used to the idea that I was going to be a mom."

"I'm so sorry," I choked out, pressing my lips to her forehead.

"It's okay," she whispered, wiping away the fat tears from her red splotched face. She looked beautiful. "I'm fine. I'm going to be fine." Damn, she was a hard ass woman, not wanting anyone to see her weak side. I would be damned if she hid that side from me.

"No, it's not okay," I replied, cupping her face so that I could make her look into my eyes. "What did the doctor say? Are *you* okay…physically?" I didn't even need to ask about her mentally. You just had to look at her to tell something wasn't right.

"I'm fine," she responded, taking a shaky breath. "It was a complete miscarriage. The baby…it wasn't viable for life. He…she…it wasn't strong enough. *I* wasn't strong enough to carry her."

"No, baby," I gasped, rocking her in my arms. "You were strong. Please don't think this was your fault." I kissed the top of her head, repeating phrases of love and strength.

"Sometimes…I do think it was my fault," she admitted. "I still wonder."

"Did the doctor say you shouldn't try again?" I had to ask, needing to know the answers…the answers I should've been around to hear straight from the doctor who treated her.

"No," she said. "He said I was perfectly fine. I should be okay to try again when I'm ready."

"Thank God," I whispered. "I'm so sorry, Cora."

We sat in silence for a while, just holding each other. I let her cry on me, keeping watch for anyone that might be heading toward the bus. Kane had sent everyone away and told them not to return to the bus until he gave them the okay.

We both knew that Coraline would be humiliated if anyone on the crew saw her breakdown. She was the strongest woman I had ever met, and she didn't like to show weakness. Her attack barely more than a day before had taken a toll on her, but she'd powered through her concussion and battered face to show the people she worked with and called family that she was tough enough to keep the show moving.

Losing herself to an emotional breakdown with me was not what I'd expected, but damn if I wasn't relieved that she let me in enough to trust me with her fragile heart. Holding her through her tears was something I vowed to do every day for the rest of my life if that was what she needed. Did it mean I loved her? Hell, I didn't even know how to recognize what love was. I had never been in a normal relationship, ever. I was always too busy partying and sleeping around with any tramp that would let me fall between her legs.

Almost killing myself by snorting too much cocaine cured me of my partying ways. Feeling like my heart could explode in my chest was the wakeup call I'd needed to change my outlook on life. Seeing my best friends, my bandmates, slowing killing themselves too? Well, we needed a change. It was a miracle that we all made the decision together. Minus our ex-drummer who was now behind bars.

My drug use over the years came flashing back in a rush. Did the baby not survive because my sperm were fucked up? *Fuck!* Was this my fault? Coraline was healthy and vibrant and beautiful. There was no way this was her fault. It had to be mine…

My phone rang, disrupting our moment. I cursed when I saw it was my bandmate and lead singer of *Fatal Cross*.

"Hey, Ace," I said, greeting him with more enthusiasm than I felt. "What's going on?"

"Hate to bother you, man, but I needed to let you know," he sighed. "We just fired Jose."

"What? Why?" I asked, shocked at his words. Jose was the guy who'd been our tour manager for the past six years.

"He was arrested last night," Ace fumed. "He's been selling drugs when he wasn't working for us. Looks like he was deep in the drug trade here in Seattle. They found a few hundred thousand dollars of coke in his house. He's going to be put away for a long time."

"Son of a bitch!" I roared. How many people did we know that had their finger in the very thing we were trying to stay away from? "I swear, we are going to have to start doing drug tests on our crew."

"That very thought has crossed my mind," he agreed. "I called because we need to find a new tour manager, like yesterday, man. We leave for London in two weeks. I know you will be over there already, but I need your help in finding a replacement."

My eyes locked with Cora's and she was already shaking her head, but I ignored her. She'd planned on a lengthy vacation after this tour, but I wasn't going to let her get away from me this time. She wasn't going to run…no, not this time. I had to keep a strong hold on her or she'd leave me in her dust as she found a secluded place somewhere on this planet to sulk in her own self-induced exile.

"I'll get back to you," I said, hanging up the phone after a promise to call him back soon.

"No," she protested. "I like my quiet time. I need a break, Taylor."

"I'm not giving you an option, Cora," I demanded, using my knuckle to direct her chin back in my direction. She squirmed to get out of my lap, but I locked my other arm around her tightly. She wasn't going to run from me this time.

"You can't make me go," she cursed. "Taylor, please. Don't make me…I can't."

"Can't what?" I questioned, looking deep into those hazel eyes that hid so much, but also showed so much pain.

"I can't be around you," she mumbled softly, tightening the hold around her stomach. "It…hurts too much."

"I know it does, baby," I said, pressing my forehead to hers. I felt her shoulders begin to shake and I knew she was about to break down again. "I'm not asking you, Coraline Maddox. I'm *telling* you that you will work for me on this next tour. It's time we work things out. You and I both know that being apart doesn't work for either of us."

"You sound so sure of yourself," she chimed in, but I saw the relief in her eyes. She was going to cave and come to work for us.

"You know I'm right," I flirted, cupping the side of her face. I peered into her eyes and did the one thing that I'd wanted to do ever since I pinned her to the side of the bus when I first got here.

I finished the kiss I started when she ran away from me.

Her lips were just as soft and warm as I remembered. There was a salty taste to the bottom one when I bit it to demand she open for me. On her gasp, my tongue invaded her mouth; tasting, plundering, and marking her as mine. She only protested for a second. Once I deepened the kiss, she melted into my embrace. By the time we parted, she was panting just as heavily as I was, her tiny body formed against my chest as if she was made for me.

"Come on, baby," I said, kissing the tip of her nose. "Let me feed you and then we can get to work. You have another tour to prepare for."

I didn't give her the option of telling me no.

CHAPTER 13

Coraline

It was the first night of the tour with *Fatal Cross*. The band had met up with us the night before to watch *Glory Days* perform their final show on their tour. Kane and my guys were heading home to be with their wives and to welcome Gabe's new baby girl into the family.

Kane had left reluctantly. Doug was still on the run, and my cousin didn't like the fact that *Fatal Cross* didn't have actual security guards on staff. They had their crew, who doubled as crowd control. Kane wanted to leave a guy with me, but Taylor promised that no one would touch me; he swore it on his life.

Taylor's band was big, but nothing like my cousin's band. I had a feeling that they would be thrust into the spotlight in no time at all. If they kept pumping out songs like what were on their newest album, they'd be selling out arenas before the end of the year.

There was a small crew that worked for *Fatal Cross*. Three men arrived by way of a rented tour bus just an hour ago. This was the only bus they needed because of how small their crew was that worked for them. We'd all be sharing a bus. There were eight bunks and an extra living space in the back where the bus I was used to riding on had a bedroom.

When the band arrived, I was passed around with hugs and thanks for saving them by agreeing to work on such a short notice. I didn't tell them that I didn't have a choice. Taylor wouldn't allow me to be anywhere else.

After my breakdown, we worked side by side in comfortable silence. Nothing else was said about the baby or him not calling. I could tell it still bothered him that he wasn't there for me when I needed him most. He was more quiet than usual and there was something in his eyes that hadn't ever been there before…guilt.

The kiss he'd planted on me, after he *told* me I was working for them, set my body on fire. All of the work I did to forget Taylor Vaughn was gone after that moment of passion. Now, while I helped set up the stage, I tried my hardest to stay low and not dwell on the spark that fired up when we touched.

Josh, their sound guy, waved to get my attention. I stretched my back as I climbed out from under Braxton's kit. The new drummer for *Fatal Cross* was standing in the shadows, watching us work. Taylor said that the huge guy was a softie, but he honestly scared me when he growled at the other men. He kept a wide birth around me and didn't speak more than a few one or two word answers.

"I'm ready for sound check when everyone gets back from eating lunch, Cora," Josh smiled. I liked this guy. He was older, maybe in his mid-forties, and had been with the band through thick and thin. I'd hung out with him on the tours they'd been on with *Glory Days*. Josh was the only one who'd stuck around during the hiatus the band took while they all went through drug rehab.

The other two guys, Liam and Kevin, were brothers and so close in age that they could pass for twins. They were also Josh's sons. All of the Forrest men were charming and worked as hard as myself. They all sported short cropped black hair. Although, Josh's had a little gray dusting right around his temples. Their sharp blue eyes would melt any woman that crossed their paths, and if it wasn't for a certain guitarist, I'd be a little flattered at their flirting.

Taylor, on the other hand, was grumpy as hell at the two sons who were right around my age. If he caught us talking, he grumbled something low and menacing, sending them scurrying away with their tails tucked between their legs.

"Come on, Josh," I said. "Let's go grab something to eat while we have a moment. The boys can pick up where we left off."

"You got it, darlin'," he smiled, draping an arm over my shoulders. "I hope they left us enough."

"You never know," I laughed. "It's good to see you are still with these guys."

"It's good to have you along for the tour this time," he grinned, ruffling my hair as we pushed our way into the backstage area. "The other guy wasn't pulling his weight."

"That's what I hear," I replied, entering the green room.

Grant "Ace" Ryker was asleep on the couch, a baseball cap pulled over his eyes. He'd put himself on a self-imposed vocal rest hours before the show, saying he didn't want to blow his voice out like he'd done in the past.

Cash Roberts, the bassist, was on the phone with someone, speaking quietly so that he wasn't heard. Braxton had made his way back, following behind us as we entered the room. He smiled softly at me as he waited until I filled my plate.

I grabbed a slice of cheese and ham, adding a few grapes to my plate. It shocked me for a moment when Braxton placed his hand on my forearm and said, "You need to eat more than that, little bit. You're too tiny as it is."

It took me a moment to get over the shock of his concern for my eating habits. The man hadn't paid much attention to me since he arrived earlier in the day. Well, except for making sure I didn't sabotage his drum kit.

"Thank you, Brax," I smiled, giving him his own nickname. "I really don't eat much."

"Taylor needs to take better care of his woman," Braxton grunted, his massive shoulders flexing beneath the ripped up shirt advertising a national chain workout facility. I scowled at his back as he walked over to the cooler to grab a bottled water. I didn't think that I was Taylor's woman.

Speaking of Taylor, where the hell was he? Josh was over in the corner, talking to his sons and instructing them on what was left to be done before the other bands showed up. I took a seat at a small pub table and lifted myself up onto the tall stool. I had to hop a little to get myself seated. Sometimes it really sucked being so short.

Just as I sat down, Taylor walked in looking like sex on a stick. He wore a thin, white shirt that stretched across his broad shoulders. His jeans were faded and rode low on his hips. His eyes brightened when he saw me sitting at the table, but when they took in the plate, he frowned. Turning for the food table, he quietly filled a plate and grabbed his own drink out of the cooler.

"You need to eat more than that," he scolded, rolling some grapes and a few pieces of strawberries onto my plate.

"I'm really not that hungry," I shrugged.

"Are you feeling okay?" he asked, taking a seat across from me. He raised a brow, waiting for me to reply.

"Yes," I smiled, popping a strawberry into my mouth. "I'm fine, Taylor."

His eyes searched my face for a few seconds, before nodding and then digging into what was left on his plate.

"Everything okay with you?" I asked, reaching for his free hand. He stopped eating and looked up at me through those deliciously long lashes of his.

"It's fine," he said, turning his hand over so that he could squeeze my fingers gently.

He still looked tired, like he wasn't quite over the jetlag. I didn't say anything to him, but I was worried that the stress of the new tour would take a toll on him. He'd been clean for just over two years, but he'd told me a few times that sometimes the cravings were there and those days were the hardest.

How was I supposed to know when he was having one of those days? I wanted to help him beat this, but I didn't know how. I didn't know if I was even capable of giving him what he needed. I'd never even tried drugs when I was younger. My cousin kept me away from the people in our neighborhood who preyed on the young kids, offering them a little taste. Kane had done his fair share of drugs when he was younger and he didn't want me going down that destructive road. Maybe I needed to research drug addiction when I had some time to myself?

"Cora?" Josh called out from the door. "You ready?"

"Yes," I smiled, slipping off the stool. I ran my fingers over Taylor's forearm to get his attention. "Come find me if you just want to hang until the show, okay?" I didn't know what else to say or do. Maybe, just maybe, he'd open up to me. I hated seeing him this way.

"Sure, baby," he smiled, but it didn't reach his eyes.

Josh and I worked diligently through the sound check and had the guys ready to perform in no time at all. I grabbed my bag by the soundboard and made my way out to the bus. The back of the venue was cordoned off by a chain link fence, blocking out the fans who'd already gathered at the side of the building waiting for the doors to open.

The opening bands had finally showed up and it was my turn to take a break before I was needed again. That gave me about three hours before the actual set time for *Fatal Cross*.

As I boarded the bus, I squealed as strong, warm hands enveloped me. "Taylor," I sighed, letting him bury his face into my neck. I was so much shorter than him, so he had to bend at the waist to hold me close to his body. His muscular arms were like steel bars as they wrapped around my body, lifting me up. My legs automatically wrapped around him as he carried me to the back of the bus.

"What's wrong, Taylor?" I worried. "Talk to me."

"I just need to hold you for a minute," he mumbled into my neck. "Please, just let me…"

He was struggling with his demons, and I had no idea how to bring him out of the darkness he had fallen into over the past few days. I was just relieved that he was holding me, instead of trying to find another more dangerous way to cope with the events that had led us to where we were in that moment.

I rubbed absently on the shaved spot over his left ear, hoping my comforting touch soothed him. His body shuddered with each stroke of my finger. My own body melted into his strong hold when I felt his warm lips press to the spot below my ear.

"Please, Cora," he whispered, before biting down on my earlobe. "Let me get lost in you. I need you."

I knew that I shouldn't be here. Our history put us both at risk. Taylor was trying to forget his demons, and I was trying to protect my heart. He needed this, but at what cost to me? We'd already found out the hard way that our desires for each other could be fatal. It couldn't ever work out between us, but *fuck*, I wanted this…needed him as much as he needed me.

There were no words spoken as his lips laid a blazing trail from my neck to the line of my jaw. I panted heavily and my body stiffened. He pulled back slightly, and when his eyes fell on mine, I saw everything that made Taylor Vaughn the man who'd stolen my heart on that island. I saw the pain that radiated through him from the guilt of not being there for me when I needed him the most.

And that alone pushed me to accept the heated kiss that came next.

His eyes closed at the moment our lips touched. His contented sigh had my hands going to his shirt, tugging it up his back. We parted momentarily so that he could rip it over his head, tossing it on the floor.

My breasts felt weighted as he pressed his huge palm to my back, pulling me closer to his body. We pulled back from the kiss so that we could catch our breath. His eyes darkened with need, desire, and lust. My own hazel eyes were wet with unshed tears. He noticed and buried his face in my neck again, and I quickly realized that was the place where he felt safe and secure.

His hands skimmed down my sides, ducking under my tank top in the back. I felt the catch release on my bra, my nipples tingled with anticipation of his touch. He growled softly when he stripped my shirt and bra off in one swift movement.

Lips, hot and soft as velvet, landed on the spot between the two. He kissed and licked a path to my right breast, taking the hardened nipple between his teeth. I threw my head back and pushed my pussy closer to the hardness behind the fly of the denim jeans he was wearing. The slight bite of pain had me grinding myself against him, needing the friction on that spot that wept for him.

It felt amazingly right, here in his arms, but the more reasonable side of me wanted to run. Could we ever be good for each other? Would Taylor self-destruct if I couldn't handle a relationship with him? Hell, would *I* be able to let him go?

His thumb replaced his mouth, rubbing circles around the peak. He pushed my body backwards so that I was almost resting against the top of his legs. I buried my fingers into the hair on top of his head to hold me in place as he kissed another trail down the center of my stomach, stopping to nip the soft flesh below my belly button.

I gasped out in shock when he suddenly stood, holding me close to his bared chest. Skin to skin, my nipples ached as they rubbed against the smoothness of his chest. One of them grazed his nipple piercing and I felt my pussy flood with desire. He tucked my face into the crook of his neck so that he could look over my shoulder as he walked us toward the bunks.

I didn't ask him what he was doing. I'd never let a man rule me, but trusting Taylor enough to know he'd never let anything or anyone intentionally hurt me was as easy as breathing. Giving up control to him was a secret only he and I knew to be true. It was the only time in my life that I handed over the reins, and even he knew that was one of the hardest things for me to do.

He knelt slightly to reach into his bag that laid across his bunk. I heard the unmistakable sound of a box and foil packets, knowing damn good and well he was grabbing a condom. At least this time we were going to be responsible. I bit back a snort at the thought.

My back hit the mattress on the bunk directly across from his. This was the bunk that I'd claimed as mine before I even knew he had chosen his. I shook the words from my head that said we were more alike than I wanted to admit.

Taylor kissed a trail down to the closure of my jeans, using his warm hands to unsnap them. I raised my hips so that he could shimmy the tight material down my legs; the same legs that shook with anticipation and fear.

"Beautiful as ever," he cooed, running his finger under the waistband of my black lace panties. Goose bumps raised on the skin there, and I felt my abs automatically flex in anticipation.

"Taylor, please," I begged, reaching for the fly of his jeans. He quickly divested himself of his pants, climbing into the bunk and covering me with his warmth. The curtain was drawn, plunging us into darkness in the small sleeping area. There wasn't much room to move, but there was enough to accomplish what we were there to do.

"Tear," he demanded, pressing the foil pack against my mouth. I took the wrapper with my teeth as he pulled the end between his fingers, tearing it open. I discarded the piece left in my mouth by turning my head and puffing out a quick burst of air, sending the piece somewhere off into the darkness. I couldn't see what he was doing, but by the movement of his hand, I knew he was sheathing himself for our protection.

Fingers danced along my hipbone, moving to the spot between my legs. At the same moment he took my lips again, I felt him press a finger against the slick folds of my sex. I rotated my hips and pivoted upward so that he could slide in with ease. His thumb rotated on the swollen nub that ached for his touch with each stoke to my dripping pussy.

"You're always so wet for me, baby," he whispered in awe, releasing my lips so that he could slide down my body. He didn't go easy on me when he pushed my legs out to the side, burying his face where I yearned for him most. He ate at me like a starving man, devouring every drop of desire my body had created just for this man. I couldn't see him, but I could feel everything he was doing. Without my sense of sight, every touch…every tender lick was registering in my brain. I struggled to push his head away when the intensity grew to be too much. He growled out a warning and I obeyed him, dropping my hands to the sheet at my sides. Fisting the material, I bit my lip to keep from crying out loudly, fighting the impending release I knew was about to shatter my world.

"Come for me, Cora," he demanded. "You are mine. You've always *been* mine. I'm not letting you run from me again." His words were cut off when he buried his face into my sex.

I thrashed my head from side to side, refusing to let my body release. I wanted to let go, but I just...couldn't. There was so much rolling around inside me that I wouldn't let myself focus on what he was doing.

The night on the island.

The romantic dinner for two.

A child.

A pregnancy that didn't last.

"Shh, baby. Don't cry," he begged. I hadn't even realized that he'd climbed back up my body and was now nose to nose with me, wiping away a stray tear in the darkness. How did he know?

"I'm sorry," I apologized, forcing myself to stop the tears. "I'm sorry, Taylor."

"Let me take the pain away, please. I need you just as much," he demanded, his voice deep and commanding.

"Help me forget, Taylor," I whimpered, accepting a soft press of his lips.

"Yes, baby…anything you need," he panted, kicking my right leg out to the side so that he could fit between my legs.

"I need you," I whispered.

"Let me love you," he stated, as he took my lips again with force.

It wasn't a question or even an intention of things to come, because the next thing I felt was his hardness pressing against the opening of my sex. He'd barely pressed forward when my body opened up and accepted him like he was destined to be there.

We both swore as he seated himself to the hilt inside me. The stirrings of the climax I had tried to deny myself turned into blazing fire as he wrapped his arms around my back and buried his face in my neck, the place he found comfort.

My hips raised to meet his punishing thrusts, my nails scored his back as he increased the depth and intensity of his strokes. Our grunts and mewls of excitement only spurred him on, and I found myself raising up to meet him every time.

"Come for me, Coraline," he demanded, grabbing my tiny hand into his larger one and tucking it between our bodies. Together, we slid my fingers to my clit, rotating the area as one. As I touched myself the way I knew would help me achieve release, Taylor pressed firmly the way he remembered it drove me mad. "God, I can feel you clamping down on my cock, baby. Come on. Come for me."

"Taylor," I grunted, feeling the stirrings of an explosive release. I was so close.

"Cora," he groaned out, rotating his hips one last time before I exploded beneath him. It wasn't long before he followed behind me.

He stayed above me, kissing me and petting the side of my face as I bathed in the post-orgasmic haze of our release. I didn't want to move, because this state of peace I was in was something I'd missed since our last encounter. When he held me after sex, I knew that whatever we'd just shared wasn't just two people looking to get lost in each other for one night. The unspoken magic that flowed between us was hot as fire and dangerous as sin, and I knew that eventually, I'd fall in love with Taylor Vaughn.

That was...if I hadn't fallen in love with him already.

CHAPTER 14

Taylor

I climbed out of the bunk slowly and quietly, trying to not wake her up. She'd fallen asleep after we'd made love. She'd let me drown my sorrows into the only heaven that gave me peace anymore. She had her own demons she worked through, and I was probably the biggest asshole in the world for using sex to help myself cope with the things that were going on in my head. The guilt of not being with her when she lost the baby was the biggest one. The guilt of possibly being the reason for the baby's death was the second.

After getting a quick drink, I returned to her bunk, sliding in slowly. She was so tiny that I had plenty of room to snuggle next to her without discomfort. I closed my eyes in bliss when she wrapped a delicate arm over my chest, her thumb absently traced the cross tattoo on the left side of my ribs. I found myself rubbing the outside of her elbow with my thumb, finding more comfort in that small gesture than I should have.

Cora was a contradiction. She was tiny, but she was also as strong as an ox. She'd worked with her cousin for several years, choosing not to go on to college. I'm sure Kane paid her more than any other tour manager I'd met. She was well worth the money. I knew that I couldn't steal her away to work for *Fatal Cross*, but I was going to try.

I laughed to myself, imagining how that would so not go over well.

A little voice in the back of my head said that it could happen if I made her mine.

My thoughts were interrupted when her body jerked awake. She gasped, cursed, and pushed at my shoulders, "Oh shit! Get up, Taylor! I have to get back to work. Why the hell did you let me sleep?"

"Because you were so content and soft," I smiled, kissing her lips. I had to pull away or we'd have missed the show because we were too consumed with being tied up together, burning up the sheets.

"Work first," she scolded as she climbed over my body…naked. "Playtime later."

"Hey!" I barked, grabbing her arm and looking around the bus to make sure there was no one around to see her naked.

"What?" she asked, confused, cocking her head to the side.

"You're naked," I snarled, very possessively.

"So?" she shrugged.

"Someone could've seen you, Cora," I admonished, glaring at her. She had no idea how I would kill one of the guys if they ever saw her naked.

"It's not like they've never seen a naked woman," she laughed, rolling her eyes. That woman was too damned independent for her own good.

"And they will never see you naked," I promised. "Or I'll kill them…dead."

"Come on, grumpy pants, we have work to do," she smirked, pulling a tank top over her head and sliding into her jeans. She pushed me toward the front of the bus, hopping on my back as I descended the stairs and giggling as I bounced her as I walked.

Braxton was standing by the back door, watching the bus intently. I didn't say anything to Cora, but she noticed. I felt her stiffen on my back. "Why is he always watching people?" she whispered.

"He's always been that way, but he's a good guy, Cora," I said quietly, not thinking it was my place to say anything about our silent drummer. "He's loyal and protective of everyone. He's the type of guy you want on your side."

I felt her nod and relax, tightening her hold around the top of my shoulders. My drummer slid in the door and didn't acknowledge us as we approached the building. I let her slide down my back before we walked through the door.

"Thank you for staying on board with us," I said, pulling her to my chest. "I'm glad you said yes."

"Me, too," she smirked, standing on the tips of her toes so she could place a loud, smacking kiss to my lips. She pulled the door open and bounced inside, throwing a wink over her shoulder. "Even if you didn't give me the option to say no."

The sexy sway to her hips had my cock twitching to get back inside her sweet heaven. Damn, she was going to be the death of me.

CHAPTER 15

Coraline

Watching *Fatal Cross* on stage was always a treat. The band was harder; grungier than my cousin's band. Taylor was currently standing with his legs splayed apart, his guitar slung low across the tops of his thighs and his head thrown back with his eyes closed tight while playing their newest single.

His jeans hugged his ass perfectly, and I knew this because he'd just turned to walk away from my spot at the side of the stage. My mind wandered back to just a few hours ago when my nails were deep in those firm muscles as he brought me so much pleasure.

I looked up just as he was walking back to my side of the stage, sending me a flirtatious wink in the process. Damn, he was so handsome…beautiful even.

The stage darkened and the lights flashed red as the hiss from the fog machine sounded beside me. The fog would roll in from the side of the stage and the red lights would catch it, making it look like the fog had turned to blood. This next song was dark, twisted almost. To some, the lyrics would make you believe it was about some supernatural force, but I knew it was about the horrors of drug addiction. This song was one of their number one hits off of the last album.

The mic at my shoulder crackled, Liam calling out for my help at the merchandise booth. "Cora, I need your help. They've wiped me out of large shirts. Can you be a dear and bring a box?"

I clicked the button to open the line and laughed, "The show's not even over yet and you've run out?"

"You don't even know, girl," he chuckled. "Get your butt back here."

"On my way," I replied, casting one last glance over my shoulder at the sexy guitarist.

I pushed the doors open and exited the backstage area, pressing myself against the wall. Bodies were packed tight, and I couldn't move as fast as I wanted to with everyone stepping on my feet. If I was a little taller, I probably wouldn't be having to fight my way through the crowd. It'd been a long time since I had dealt with the smaller venues that Kane's band used to play, and I'd forgotten how tightly packed the fans would be during the concert.

"Took you long enough," Liam teased, winking in my direction as he handed over a shirt to a guy in line.

"Thank God I'm wearing steel toed boots," I smirked, pointing toward my feet. "Or I'd be in a world of hurt right now."

By the time I arrived at the table, there was a line of people piling up to grab shirts, even though the show was in full force. I directed the line to break into two rows and got down to selling shirts and CD's, laughing and cutting up with the fans. The overseas crowds always showed up en masse. I'd noticed several people in the crowd with some older *Fatal Cross* shirts from the tour a few years ago. That was the one they'd been on right before entering rehab and getting their shit together.

The music stopped and I looked up at the stage. Ace was talking to the people in the audience and Taylor was standing at his place behind the mic, looking out across the crowd, a worried expression marring his brow. He glanced over his shoulder at Braxton, who was behind the drum kit, downing a bottle of water. Something was said between the two and the quiet drummer motioned toward my direction. I saw Taylor squint to look out past the lights that were illuminating the band. I raised my hand to catch his eye, and when he relaxed, I knew that I'd been seen. My heart also skipped a beat at the knowledge that Taylor Vaughn was looking out for me.

The lines died down enough that Liam took a quick break to grab a drink and a smoke. I laughed with a few guys who'd come over to buy some shirts. They'd been to every *Fatal Cross* concert that'd come through London and they told me about how much they enjoyed this one the most.

Liam returned and I was able to sneak away just as the band had begun their last song in the set. I found myself watching them again. Ace, with his wild curls now draped completely in sweat, and Cash, with his long blonde hair, worked the stage alongside Taylor. He'd just turned his head to sing his portion of the backup vocals when he noticed I was standing to his right. I was so close that I could see his beautiful eyes sparkle as he sang directly to me, instead of the crowd. I didn't even hear what the lyrics were as I found myself lost in his eyes.

Before I knew it, the show ended and the guys were coming off stage. I handed each of them towels to dry off their hair and faces. I held out my hand for their ear pieces, and Josh had just stepped up to take the guys' guitars when Taylor wrapped an arm around my waist, pulling me close for a chaste kiss to the lips.

"Get changed," I said, pushing Taylor away gently. "You have a ton of people out there. How long do you want to sign autographs before I pull you away?"

"Give us an hour," Cash said, pulling his hair up into a sloppy ponytail. "Then get us out."

"Gotcha," I grinned. "I'll go set up while you guys wind down for a few minutes. I'll give you twenty before I come back to escort you out."

"Thanks, Cora," everyone sang out, making me smile. This was my job, and one I took great pride in.

Fans were pushed back behind barriers, and Kevin had just moved two long tables around so that the band could come straight from the backstage area to their seats without being mauled. When I looked into the crowd of waiting fans, I chuckled to myself. It was going to take longer than an hour to get everyone through the line.

I got the attention of the crowd by standing on one of the folding chairs. I was small and it was the only way to get people to see me. I'd been doing this for a long time.

"Alright," I yelled, getting everyone's attention. What I lacked in height, my voice made up for the difference. "Are you guys ready to meet *Fatal Cross*?" I laughed loudly when the crowd roared with excitement. "I ask that you keep to the line and do not take too long with each band member. Photos are welcomed and they will sign anything you want. Thank you!"

With that, I climbed down and grabbed Liam, leaving Josh and Kevin to stand guard at the table, one on each end. One of the female bartenders dropped a bucket of ice water on the bar as I passed, nodding as I said my thanks. I grabbed the handle and made my way to the private room in the back.

"Ready?" Taylor asked, coming up to my side. He'd changed out of his sweaty clothes and now wore a pair of black jeans and a gray cotton shirt that stretched tight across his massive chest. The little barbells in his nipples were outlined in the material. Damn, I really need to stop looking at him while I worked.

"Let's go," Braxton said, holding the door open for everyone to pass through.

As we approached the table, the crowd cheered for the guys, flashes of light causing my eyes to blink rapidly to keep from going blind. A woman called out Ace's name and I smiled when he looked at the woman, giving her a saucy wink.

Josh laid out markers for the guys, and before the line started moving, Taylor grasped my hand, pulling me down so he could whisper in my ear, "Don't move from my side."

"Okay," I replied, watching his features closely. He didn't like the fact that I was so tiny in such a big crowd. He'd said that the first time they'd toured with my cousin's band. Kane and the guys had told him that I could hold my own, but Taylor still didn't like me being in a situation that could cause me to get harmed.

Braxton was on my left at the end of the table, while Taylor was on my right. Cash was on the other side of Taylor, and Ace brought up the end so that he was the first to meet the fans. It was easier that way, because the singer was always the most popular.

The guys worked the crowd of around fifty people. They'd paid good money to hang around after the show to meet the band. I ended up being the one to take the photographs as fans handed me their phones.

Taylor kept an eye on me during their meet and greet, moving his body to shield me as two guys checked me out a little creepily. They meant no harm, but I was beginning to notice Taylor was a tad more protective since we'd made love on the bus earlier.

He'd told me that I was his, and I would be lying if I said that it bothered me, because it didn't. I wanted to be his, because he was mine. I'd fought this for too damn long, and being without him…well, let's just say it didn't work. When I was with him, I felt whole…I felt more like myself. I needed him in my life, even though things started out on the wrong foot.

"Sorry," a fan said, bumping into my side. They guy was drunk, but at least he was polite. I heard Taylor growl as he rushed forward.

"I'm okay," I reassured him, placing a calming hand on his forearm. When I looked into his eyes, they'd darkened as he glared at the fan who'd continued on his way out of the building along with several of his buddies.

"Are you sure?" he inquired as he checked me over, rubbing his hands up and down my arms, but still glaring at the door as if he thought the fan would make another appearance.

"Taylor," I said forcefully, squeezing his arm to get his attention. "Taylor! Look at me."

"Sorry," he muttered, finally making eye contact. "What is it, baby?"

"I'm okay," I told him gently, glancing at the remaining fans who were not paying attention to us, because Cash and Ace were keeping them occupied until Taylor could get back to his seat.

"I don't like seeing you hurt," he smiled, taking my chin with his thumb and forefinger, giving it a slight lift so that I'd look up into his eyes.

"I'm fine," I grinned back. "Now, get to work."

"Yes, ma'am," he winked, before swooping down to place a soft kiss to my lips. A few people in the crowd clapped loudly when they saw our exchange. Taylor returned to his seat, but held his hand out behind him, reaching out for my touch. When our fingers connected, I felt like I was coming home.

As the crowd finished talking with the band, Liam and Josh pushed everyone back so that I could escort the guys toward the back of the stage and out to the bus. "I'm going back in to break everything down. You guys relax. Is there anything you need from me before I go?"

"No, Cora, but thank you," Cash responded. He'd put his long hair up into a sloppy man ponytail, groaned, and took a seat on the black leather couch. "Are you sure we can't steal you away from your cousin?"

"That would not go over very well," I frowned, seeing hurt flash across Taylor's face. I knew this would happen. I was only doing this temporarily and he knew that, but what was going to happen after this tour? I was not going to be leaving *Glory Days* to work with *Fatal Cross*. It just wasn't going to happen.

"Go finish up so we can get out of here," Taylor said, squeezing my hand as he walked toward the back of the bus. I couldn't deal with the future right now. I had work to do.

We finished fairly quickly, and the crew and Taylor stayed inside to use the shower provided by the venue while I ran out to the bus to grab my bag for when they were done. When I walked on the bus, Braxton, Ace, and Cash were already lounging around since they'd showered while I was loading up their equipment.

"I'm going in to shower before we head out," I announced, pulling my bag out of my bunk. "Everything is wrapped up with the venue, so I'll tell the driver to be ready to go in thirty minutes."

"Thanks, Cora," everyone chimed in. I smiled and left the bus, hurrying inside so that I could shower and be in the bunk as soon as the wheels started turning on the bus. I was still suffering from jetlag, and we had a long drive to our next destination.

Once I was showered and everyone was either on their computers or already asleep in their bunks, I slid the curtain back on my bunk and gasped in shock. I had to cover my mouth to stifle the giggle that came next when Taylor wrapped a muscular arm around my waist and hauled me across his chest.

"Shh, I'm kidnapping you," he cooed, kissing the spot just below my earlobe. I shivered from the contact and he noticed. "Are you cold, baby?"

"A little," I lied. Damn, he smelled amazing, and all I wanted to do was get lost in his touch, but not with six other people on the bus besides us…seven if you counted the driver.

"Sleep," he ordered, tucking me into his side and pulling the blanket up over our bodies. I wrapped my arm around his chest and tangled my leg over his. I placed a kiss to his warm skin and fell asleep in the arms of the only man I ever wanted to hold me close.

CHAPTER 16

Taylor

We'd been back in the States for twenty-four hours, and I'd had practically no time at all alone with Coraline. She'd been too busy to take any time off to spend alone with me. Kicking off our tour, we'd arrived in New York earlier in the day, and were rushed to the radio station for interviews. I was itching to get back to the bus so that I could check on her. She'd been dragging ass by the time we landed and said that she would sleep after the show tonight.

Several fans stood around as we exited the building, screaming our names as we piled into the SUV the station let us use to get to the interview. Ace stopped and signed several autographs while we piled in the back. The driver waited patiently for him to be done.

"Damn," Ace laughed, climbing into his seat. "We really need to think about getting better security. This is blowing up in our faces, boys."

"Number one on the charts," Cash cheered. It was true. Our first single had knocked our friends, *Glory Days*, out of the top spot for the past two weeks and our lives were quickly changing. We'd been contacted to pick up a few festivals in the spring, and the interview requests were pouring in for the cities on this tour. Ticket sales have skyrocketed.

"It's what we deserve," I declared. "We've worked hard for this."

"Yes we have," Braxton agreed. The normally quiet one of the bunch gave us a rare smile before schooling his features back into the hardened mask.

"Has anyone heard from *Witch's Spawn*?" Ace grumbled. "I've left messages and still…nothing. They're supposed to be at the venue already."

"Let me text Cora," I offered, pulling out my phone. After a quick message, she responded immediately that the opening band was already there and that they were unloading as we spoke.

"She said they are there and are doing their load in," I announced. Ace was a ball of nerves with this new band. Apparently, the lead singer was a friend of friend, and since we'd never met beforehand, he was more than nervous about the new lineup. We had another smaller band to round out the three bands on the bill, but they were local, and this would be their first show. After tonight, they'd pack up their RV and follow us for the next ten cities, where we'd pick up another new band.

The drive to the venue took well over half an hour, and by the time we arrived, Cora was just paying the pizza delivery man for our meal. She was trying to balance several boxes of pizza and two plastic bags weighted down with bottled sodas.

"Give me those," I said, pulling the boxes out of her hand.

"I don't see how the hell you could see over those boxes to even walk," Braxton laughed, taking the bags from the tips of her tiny fingers.

"What is this? Pick on Coraline day?" she frowned. "I didn't need help."

"Sure," Braxton teased, jumping out of the way when she tried to slap his arm. It was nice to see Braxton opening up to her. It made me feel like my family was accepting her. Well, my band family. My blood family will undoubtedly love her, I'm sure. We'll find that out in a few weeks when we stop in Kansas City for our show. It was my home town, before Seattle, and my parents still live there with my baby sister. She is married and expecting her first child. She and her husband will also be coming to the show.

As we entered the green room, *Witch's Spawn* was already sitting around, waiting for us to arrive. Their lead singer was a woman, and a friend of Kane's wife. As I looked over at Ace, I saw our fearless leader stuck in a heated stare with the lead singer. I tossed Cora a knowing look and she just shook her head and stepped forward to make introductions.

Presley Pittman smiled and shook everyone's hand, but lingered on Ace's introduction with a slight blush to her cheeks. The woman seemed to catch herself and harden her features, before introducing the rest of her band. All three guys, Brian, Drake, and Garrison, stood up to shake our hands. Brian was their drummer, and immediately struck up a conversation with Braxton. Drake was their guitarist, and Garrison was their bassist.

And I wanted to rip his fucking hands off and beat his eyes with them.

The man must've already known Cora, because he pulled her into a hug that was far from brotherly. When he buried his face into her neck, I made my move. That was *my* neck he was touching and *my* woman he was eye fucking with no shame.

"Taylor," Cora warned, but disguised it as an introduction, "this is Garrison Hale."

"Taylor Vaughn," I grunted out, wrapping a possessive arm over Cora's shoulder. The guy was quick witted, stepping back when he noticed my hold on my girl. He shook my hand and moved away to meet the other guys.

"That was just mean," she scolded.

"No," I scoffed. "That was me not killing him."

After introductions, I grabbed Cora's hand and slipped outside to the bus. The guys knew where the hell I was going, and it was imperative I had some one on one time with my girl.

"Taylor," she protested slightly as I picked her up, wrapping her legs around my waist. I pressed my hand to her lower back and then slipped the other into the short hair at the back of her head. My kiss was nothing but possessive. The feral need to claim her and mark her as my own stunned even me.

My boots pounded heavily on the path leading up the stairs of the bus and down the aisle, toward the back room. I bypassed the bunks and took her to the lounging area where I could close and lock the door. The snick of the lock signified more than us needing privacy; it was me closing out the world. I needed her. I couldn't play the good guy any longer.

Coraline Maddox was *mine*!

Grasping the black tank top with my hands, it didn't take much to tear the material, ripping it down the front. Her gasp of alarm was short lived when I buried my face between her tits. My tongue snaked out and traced the swell of each breast while my fingers flicked the front closure, allowing the cups to fall open. I didn't even bother pushing the straps off of her shoulders.

"Taylor," she pleaded, grasping the hair on the top of my head. "Please…"

"You don't have to beg, baby," I panted. "Never beg me for anything."

"Yesssss," she hissed, as I pushed her back onto the plush leather couch. Tiny track lights in the ceiling and along the base of the seats were the only things illuminating the room. I pulled her boots off after cursing the damn laces, swearing I would buy her slip-ons before the next show. Her jeans came off in one quick tug, because I didn't want to destroy all of her clothes.

The black lace panties were nothing more than shredded material in my hands.

"*Fuck*," I growled, swiping my tongue up her heated lips. "You're so wet for me like always."

"Yes," she huffed out, pushing her pussy closer to my mouth. Greedy little woman…I liked it!

I had to throw my arm over her waist to keep her still. "If you don't quit moving, I will tie you down to this couch." It really did no good. She was in the throes of our passion already, and I didn't think anything I said would stop her from accepting the pleasure I was planning for her.

"Please, Taylor," she cried out.

"You are to do as I say, Coraline," I demanded, feeling my body tighten in response to her taste. "You've been away from me for too long."

"I've been here," she giggled.

"Come here," I said, pulling her to her feet. I didn't waste time with words. I'd dreamed about that smart little mouth around my cock for months!

Pushing her to her knees, I noticed the small smirk at the corner of her lips as I took charge. She'd told me on that island that she'd been in control of every aspect of her life, and giving up control to me was what she needed...to just let go of everything, lose control for once in her life.

Pulling my cock free, I groaned as her tiny tongue snaked out and wet her lips in a seductive swipe. She reached up and folded her fingers over the base of my cock as her eyes heated with desire. I fell back on the couch and threaded my fingers into her short black hair, pulling her toward my awaiting length.

"Take me...all of me, baby," I demanded, watching as she swallowed my cock. "Jesus...fuck."

"Mmmm," she moaned, causing my balls to tighten, just begging for release. I had to squint my eyes to keep from ending this before we even got started. Her tongue danced around the head and, after several passes, I was about to come unglued.

The back of her throat tightened when she took all of me. I wanted to release in her mouth, but I held back, telling myself that I needed her pussy tonight. With each pass of her mouth, I felt my need to be buried inside her grow.

"On your knees, Cora. On the couch, and hold on to the back," I snarled, pulling her mouth away from my cock. That was one of the hardest things I had ever done. That woman had a wickedly talented mouth, and I was an idiot to stop her, but I wanted inside her warmth.

When she was where I wanted her, I entered her in one swift movement, folding myself over her back so that I could kiss the top of her shoulder. Her heat wrapped around me, pulling me deeper inside. I drove deep, fast…slow. Every movement I made increased the mewling coming from her mouth. At one point, I had to wrap my arm around her waist to keep her from falling forward. There was no way in hell I was going to let her give out now.

"Oh, God, don't stop. Please don't stop, Taylor," she chanted, pushing back to meet me thrust for thrust. Her pussy clamped down just as she cried out in release. "More…"

I didn't stop thrusting deep, giving her what she needed…what she craved. I fought off my own release to give her what she wanted. I know it took every ounce of willpower in her body to give up the control so she could just…feel.

"Are you on the pill?" I growled, leaning in close to her ear. Her panting had subsided somewhat, but her pussy still dripped for me. "I want to come inside you. I need to know, Cora."

"Yes," she cried out, but not in passion. Her body stiffened and I felt my heart stop dead in my chest. "But…I was…before."

Just as quickly as my passion rose for her, my heart exploded with pain as tears sprung forth from her eyes. But it was no use. I was too late.

My cock pulsed, emptying my seed inside her once again.

CHAPTER 17

Coraline

"No!" he roared, tightening his hold around my waist. What the hell was I supposed to do? He didn't protect himself when he had me bent over. I should've told him. I should've been more responsible.

"I'm sorry…I'm sorry, Taylor," I panicked, pushing at his large body, but I couldn't budge him. It took all I had to keep from crawling out of my skin. Feeling him this close to me made the pain return…made my chest *hurt*. "Just…Just let me go!"

"No, Coraline!" he howled, using his massive arms to spin me around. I felt his essence between my legs when his now flaccid cock slipped free of my body. "You are not running from me, sweetheart. Not again."

"I…I can't do this," I cried, cursing myself for putting him in this situation again. "It's my

fault. I should've made you wear a condom."
His beautiful green eyes searched my face. What
was he looking for? I had no idea, but I couldn't
bring him any more pain. I could see the guilt
resurfacing in his gaze, and I couldn't let him
hurt. I'd already done enough of that for the
both of us.

"It's my fault," he whispered, more himself
now. I knew his yelling was during the heat of
the moment, but it still hurt all the same. "It's
my responsibility to protect *you*. I didn't."

"I'm…," I began, but his inhuman wail cut
me off. I looked up into his eyes and I saw
pain…raw pain.

"Please, do not say you are sorry," he
snapped, pulling me flush against his chest.
When he buried his face in my neck, my tears
began again, and I couldn't stop my arms from
wrapping around his broad shoulders, holding
his body against mine.

"It's going to be okay, Taylor," I murmured, placing my lips at his temple. "It's not going to happen again."

"You were on the pill then?" he was shocked, mumbling his question into my neck...the place he found peace.

"Yes," I admitted. "I don't know why...or how it happened, but it did. Maybe it was the alcohol that night, maybe it was fate, but it happened and it's over. I have to move on. *We* have to move on."

"I will never forgive myself," he paused, shaking his head. "He...the baby probably didn't survive because of all of my drug use. I'm tainted. It couldn't have been your fault."

I was stunned....completely floored at his words.

"What?" I sputtered, holding him tighter, as if I could take away his pain. "Taylor! You can't know that!"

"But it's the only reason I can come up with," he stated dejectedly, pulling his face away so I could look into his watery eyes. God, his tears killed me. "You are healthy and pure and…clean."

"It wasn't either one of our faults, Taylor," I said, stroking his face in comfort. When he nuzzled his cheek into my palm, I sighed in relief at his acceptance of the gesture. He was opening up to me, and even though we were half naked, covered in both of our combined fluids, we *were* going to have this talk. It was well past time for that.

"I should've been there for you, but I was selfish," he groaned. "If I'd just answered the damn phone."

"It's okay," I reassured him, letting him pick me up and carry me to the bunk. I didn't know how he knew that the bus was still vacant, but it was. He laid me down gently and walked away, returning quickly with a washcloth. I protested when he tried to clean his seed from between my legs.

"My job," he growled. I allowed my legs fall to the side and let him do it without another word. He turned away, and I didn't look out to see what he was doing. It wasn't long before he tossed our clothes, well mostly my clothes, in the corner of the bunk by my feet. Sliding in, he pulled me into his arms. "I want to know what happened, Coraline. I deserve to know *everything*."

He was right. I'd kept him in the dark for far too long, and it was time that we discussed what happened with the baby. He also had to come clean about why he didn't answer or even call me back. It was very hard to do, but I sucked it up, starting with the night I realized I was late in getting my period.

"I ran to the store and bought a pregnancy test," I paused, composing myself. "I took it, and when it came back positive, I went out and bought two more. When they were positive as well, I didn't know what to do, so I called you."

"I was in the studio that night," he remembered, his eyes vacant while he replayed those memories in his head.

"I understand," I sighed in defeat.

"After a few days, I was wore out from recording. The hours were long and I was focused on my work." He rearranged me so that I was against his side in the bunk. He flipped a lamp on, flooding the area with a small amount of light.

"I was trying to not think about it," I admitted. "I didn't want to accept that I was pregnant."

"The night I was going to call you back," he cursed. "Things went to shit quick."

"What happened?" I asked, needing to know.

"Someone knocked on the door, and when I answered, my dealer was standing there. He said he had some coke and wanted me to have first dibs. He actually tossed a small baggie at me and told me I could try some, on the house. He was trying to pressure me into buying a shitload of it and I told him to get the fuck out and never come back. Every time I replay the memory of that man standing on my doorstep, all I want to do was call a realtor and have my house sold before I finish with the tour. I can't live there any longer, Cora, and I have a feeling I'm going to make that call sooner, rather than later."

"What happened after that?" I kept going, hoping to hell he didn't keep the stuff his dealer offered.

"I called my sponsor. I was too wound up to answer your call. I...I didn't want you to hear me like that. I didn't want you knowing that I almost failed."

"But you didn't," I said, squeezing his hand for support.

"No, I didn't," he replied, shaking his head at the memory. "I packed a bag as fast as I could, locked up the house, and ran to get help."

"I'd called you the next day, too," I told him, wanting to know what happened with him. I believed him when he said that he had gone to his sponsor's house, but somehow, I had to hear the story to make it real in my head.

"I turned off my phone for a few days, and when I turned it on, I saw the missed calls, Cora," he promised, looking deep into my eyes. "I wanted so desperately to call you, but I wasn't in a good spot…my desires for a high were too intense. I didn't want any of that to touch you. I didn't want you around me when I was like that."

"It hurt," I admitted. "I'm not going to lie, Taylor. It wounded me. I tried to call you that evening, too, and got nothing."

"I was back at the studio," he answered honestly. I had no reason to not believe him. No,

Taylor Vaughn wouldn't do anything to hurt me...at least not again. "I was in the studio for a week."

"And then I stopped calling," I finished, feeling the knot of tears build in my chest. *God that hurt.*

"By then, I was not myself, Cora," he continued, "I had to stay where I could get the help I needed. I wanted so badly to get high. You don't understand the cravings of an addiction. It's like you will die without the high. Your body aches and begs and pleads with your mind...just one more time. Just one more line of coke. That'll be the last time we ever do it. That's what my mind kept playing over and over in my head. I *had* to get help before I saw you again. I couldn't bring my problems to you and your cousin's band. It was something I had to do, but if I'd known..."

"No," I interrupted, stopping him with a finger to his soft lips. "I wouldn't have let you come to my side if you needed help that badly, Taylor. I don't hate you. I don't blame you. I had Kane and Delilah. They helped me through it."

"But it should've been me," he said, pulling me closer to his chest. When I wrapped my arms across the wide expanse of his shoulders, I felt them shake with the silent sobs tearing away at his heart. "It should've been me there to hold you when you needed me the most."

"But you're here now," I pleaded, closing my eyes. "You're here now, Taylor, and that's all I need."

We stayed like that for what seemed like hours. I'd felt so torn, so confused. I wanted to hate him when he wouldn't answer my calls, but I'd forgiven him. He was struggling with something that was just as important. The whole issue needed to be put to rest, and I had to find a way to get him to forgive himself for not being there for me.

"I would've been happy for the baby," he paused, taking a deep breath. "I would've loved the little angel, Cora. I just wanted you to know that."

"Thank you," I sighed. "I know you would have."

"I still wonder…" he began, but I cut him off.

"We can't sit here and conjure up all of these what-ifs, Taylor," I said, biting my cheek to keep from crying again. I'd done enough of that to last a lifetime. "We have to move forward."

"I'm just now processing the things you've had some time to work through," he explained, placing his large hand on my stomach. "It's going to take me a bit to mourn."

"I'm so sorry," I replied, burying my face against his warm chest. He shivered when my lips made contact with his skin.

"I will never fail you again," he vowed, pushing himself up so that he could rest on his elbow and look into my eyes. "I promise you."

"I know," I whispered, cupping his face. "I know."

CHAPTER 18

Taylor

After the show that night, she fell asleep in my arms. I watched her with the small amount of light filtering through the half drawn curtain. Her long lashes were resting delicately on her cheekbones. Those soft lips I craved were pushed out into a sleepy pout. It took everything I had not to wake her up with my lips pressed to hers.

The night was met with dreams of babies with dark hair and beautiful hazel eyes. The morning also came too early, and thankfully, the bus was still moving. This meant that we hadn't quite made it to the next stop.

I slid carefully out of the bunk and made my way to the front sitting area where Ace was nursing a hot cup of coffee. He flipped through the channels on the television, cursing when he found nothing of interest to watch.

"How did last night go?" he probed. "Is Coraline okay?"

"She's fine," I sighed, placing my face in my hands; my elbows rested on my knees. "We talked. She told me everything and I told her why I never called her."

"Are you two good?" he wondered.

"Yeah," I nodded, looking up into my best friend's eyes. I saw concern and understanding, something that I needed desperately. "We are going to be okay."

Braxton stumbled out, heading straight for the coffee pot. He grumbled out something that sounded like *good morning*, and took a seat at the small table that sat three. Cash followed not long afterward.

It was another hour before I decided to wake up Coraline. If I didn't, she'd sleep all damn day. We'd learned this on the European tour just a few weeks ago. That woman could sleep a full twenty-four hours if she had the opportunity.

"Good morning, baby," I crooned, sliding into the bunk. She was curled up like a kitten with her back facing me. She batted at my hand, but I wasn't going to let her push me away. She'd done enough of that over the past few months. "Come on, Cora. You're late for work."

"Work?" she choked out, sputtering as she pushed me back. I fell on my ass in the aisle and my full-bellied laugh brought everyone over to see what the hell was going on. "Am I late?"

"No," I laughed. "But it got you up."

"You asshole!" she ranted, using her pillow to knock me upside the head. "I was sleeping!"

"I want you up," I declared, more playfully than anything else.

"Go. Away," she cursed.

"I think you need a shower," I stated, climbing to my feet. I raised a brow in her direction.

"You wouldn't!" she squeaked, backing into the bunk as far as she could go. "Taylor Vaughn, you'd better not!"

"You know I will," I teased, reaching inside for her arm. She twisted and turned, laughing loudly as I reached for any body part I could grab. When I snagged her ankle, she called me names again, but her laugh was what made me finally admit that I truly loved Coraline Maddox.

In fact, the thought stunned me so deeply that I immediately released her and climbed inside the bunk, plastering my body close to hers. My lips found the only heaven I knew…buried in her sweet neck. Her contented sigh drew me in and captured my heart.

"What's wrong?" she whispered, feeling my mood shift drastically. It wasn't what she thought. No, it was nothing like that at all. I wasn't having a moment…no, I was falling in love.

"Nothing, baby," I smiled. "Nothing at all."

"Are you two going to giggle all damn morning?" Ace called out, kicking my ass with his bare foot as he walked by the bunks. "Or are we going to grab something to eat?"

The bus stopped at a diner and we all piled inside, ordering a large breakfast. Cora took a seat next to me, her phone ringing as soon as we'd placed our order. Her cousin was calling to check in and to let her know that he'd just talked to the detective in Phoenix. We'd been so wrapped up in touring overseas that we'd forgotten all about the hired help who'd beaten her up in the back of the venue just a month ago.

"Doug is still on the loose, and Kane is worried," she filled me in, after hanging up the phone.

"We are not going to let anything happen to you," I vowed. "You just need to stay with someone. Don't be wandering off by yourself."

"Like Doug will be able to find me," she shrugged, waving her hand out to the side as if this was no big deal. "I doubt he will come around anyway."

"You are too trusting," Braxton snarled, his beefy fists clenching in anger. "You need to be watched."

"Oh, really?" she growled back.

"Yes, really," I responded, taking some of her heat off of my drummer.

"It's important that you stay with someone, Cora," Braxton interrupted, standing from his seat at the table. The dude was bigger than myself, and even after all of the muscle I regained after the years of drug use, he still outweighed me by twenty or thirty pounds. Even I knew not to mess with him when he was angry. There was something about the man that made people nervous. His constant staring and watching Coraline should have bothered me, but it didn't. He had his own demons he had to work through, and it wasn't my story to tell. Maybe someday he'd find closure for his many years of hell, but until then, I was going to keep him on my good side. If he was concerned about Coraline's safety, I wasn't going to deny him, because she could get herself into loads of trouble without even looking. The little pixie was a handful, that's for sure.

"I know this," she huffed in defeat. "I've seen it happen before with Kane's wife, Delilah. Her ex found her in New Orleans, but I just don't think Doug has the means to follow me around the country, looking for revenge."

"But he could, and that's what worries us," Ace added, giving all of us a look that said that no one was going to hurt my girl. She was family to this motley crew of misfit rockstars and we'd protect her if it came down to that asshole finding us.

"I don't like being a burden," she frowned, averting her eyes to stare at the table. "I've been doing things for myself for a very long time and it's hard to let someone else rule my world." I wasn't sure if those words were meant for more than the current subject, but she didn't have to say them for my benefit. I *knew* Coraline Maddox. She was strong, independent, and stubborn. More stubborn than anything else. The only person she'd let dictate anything in her life was her cousin Kane. He was the only true blood family she had that actually cared for her.

"Well, you're family to us, and we will take care of what's ours," Cash pledged, gaining nods from everyone around the table.

"Okay," she smiled, shakily. "Okay."

Breakfast ended and we climbed aboard the bus once again. Our next stop was in North Carolina. After that, we'd be steadily performing what would seem like every night for the next two weeks. We'd have a three day break in Missouri before doing it all over again. This was our life; one we'd chosen to live. I was just thankful that I had my dream girl with me along for the ride.

CHAPTER 19

Coraline

The next week and a half was hectic. We were now in Nashville, and I'd just left them alone in the control room at the radio station so they could do their interview with the local rock station. Josh was with me this time, because the fans had come out in droves to catch a glimpse of the band as they entered the building.

I had to smile at the increased amount of people at each stop. *Fatal Cross* was gaining popularity and I couldn't have been happier for them. They'd come a very long way in the last few years. Since they'd all gotten clean, their music had seen a huge turnaround. Ace's vocals were at their best, and the comradery between the guys was strong.

"You doing okay, Cora?" Josh had walked over to the soda machine and gotten us both bottled waters, taking a seat next to me in the row of chairs in the reception area. The station's broadcast was playing softly over the speakers throughout the building. I smiled when I heard the guys answering questions above my head, laughing and cutting up with the radio DJ's.

"Yeah," I smiled. "I'm great. Why?"

"You look tired," he pointed out, raising a brow to dare me to deny it. He was right. I *was* tired, but I also didn't want to take a break. Working was my life and all I knew how to do. I'd done nothing but take care of Kane's band since I'd graduated high school. I made damn good money and didn't need to go to college to get a degree. My cousin paid me way more than I was worth, and I was thankful for his generosity.

"I am," I said, my shoulders slumping with my admission. "It'll be okay. After this run, we will take a break and maybe, just maybe, I can sleep for two days straight."

"Thank you for coming with us," he beamed, bumping shoulders with me as he laughed. "They would've been completely lost without you. Hell, *I'd* be lost without you. I love working for them, but I couldn't handle scheduling their interviews and getting them where they needed to be on time like you do."

"Ah, thanks," I blushed, scrunching my brow. "I guess it's because I've done it for so long. It isn't that hard of a job."

"I beg to differ," he laughed loudly. "You run circles around every other tour manager I've ever seen, and you're very good at your job, Cora. I hope that you'll stay on with us for future tours." Ah, so there it was...the one thing I was trying to avoid.

"You know this is only temporary, right?" I looked at my friend, glancing away when I saw the sadness in his eyes. "I don't belong here, Josh."

"Yeah, you do," he shot back. "We need you... *Taylor* needs you." He said it. I'd thought it, but Josh said it.

"But I belong to *Glory Days*, Josh. How the hell can I split my time between both bands?" I finished my water, standing up to toss it in the trash can down the hall.

"That's not all I'm talking about and you know it, Cora," he sighed. "I can see it. Baby girl, he loves you. I've known that boy since he was a teenager. I've never seen him as happy as he is when you are near. I don't know how you are going to do it after this tour, but I'm sure you'll figure it out."

"That's what I'm afraid of," I admitted. "I don't want to leave him, but I have to do it. He lives so far away. How the hell are we going to make a relationship work when we live twelve hundred miles apart from each other?"

"You'll figure out a way," he shrugged. "It's not impossible. My wife and I have been married for twenty-seven years and we've made it work. It's hard, don't get me wrong, but it can be done. It takes two strong people to have a bond. Even with Taylor's issues, I'm sure you two will make it work."

"It's hard to see him upset," I paused, rolling my head back so I could look at the tiles on the ceiling. "I'm afraid he may relapse."

"There's always a chance for that," Josh agreed, patting my knee to get me to look at him. He waited a moment for an employee of the station to walk by. The older woman nodded politely as she passed and entered a door at the end of the hallway. "But he's been strong for this long, Cora. You can't get into the mindset that he will go get high if things don't go his way. He has to fight that battle for himself. You can support him, but don't become his only reason to stay off the drugs. He's been doing so well, and I hope to hell he doesn't relapse either. He has something to live clean for now."

"I want to help him, but I know next to nothing about addiction. He's talked about it a little," I paused, wiping a stray tear I didn't know I'd produced. The last thing I needed was to be crying when he came out of that interview.

"That's good," he smiled. "He's lucky to have you, Cora. I'm sure you'll learn as you go. That's all you can do."

"Thanks, Josh," I said, taking a deep breath to stop my chin from quivering.

"Of course," he winked. "If you and Taylor don't work out, I have two sons that are single."

"Uh, no," I laughed, slapping his upper arm as he let out a deep laugh. "Eww, Josh. They are like brothers to me."

We laughed for a few more minutes, teasing each other about his sons, whom he adored and bragged about constantly. He was a proud papa, and I was honored to call him friend.

We heard the interview coming to a close and Josh left, saying he'd bring the SUV around to be ready when the guys were done. I picked up the small box to my right and made my way back to the studio door. As I looked through the window, my eyes locked with Taylor's, and I had to smile at the way his eyes heated after only being apart for an hour. He motioned for me to come inside so I could give them the box of shirts and CDs they'd signed to leave at the station.

"Hey, Coraline," the DJ smiled. "How the hell ya been, girl?"

"Hey, Charlie," I grinned, accepting a tight hug. I didn't miss the way Taylor's nose flared at the guy touching me. Hell, I knew most of the radio people across the world, since I set up interviews for Kane's band every tour. "I'm doing great. How's the family?"

"We've been great. Michelle is pregnant...again," he beamed, pride written all over his face. I had to force myself to smile widely at his announcement. It seems like everyone I knew was fucking knocked up. I glanced at Taylor and saw the sadness swamp his features. I gave him a reassuring smile, hoping that would put him at ease.

"That's great! Congrats," I remarked, patting his back as if to say what a great job he'd done knocking up his wife. What else was I to do?

"How the hell did you boys get Coraline Maddox on your crew?" he inquired, looking toward the guys.

"I can be very persuasive," Taylor winked, causing me to laugh rather loudly.

"He's holding me against my will," I smirked.

"Well, however you got this girl," he pointed at me, raising a brow at the band. "Do *not* let her go. She's in high demand."

"No, I'm not," I rebuffed.

"Yes, you are," he teased, wrapping an arm across my shoulders as we walked out of the room and down the hallway. "I've heard other bands talking about you at several shows here in town. You are just as famous as your cousin."

"Well, I'm perfectly happy behind the scenes," I stated, accepting one last hug from the DJ. "We'll see you tonight?"

"I wouldn't miss it," he replied, heading for the door leading out of the building.

"Alright, guys. Do you want to do autographs?" I asked, peering out the window that looked over the front of the building. There was a small crowd of about forty people. A few of the employees of the station had come out to give us an extra hand with crowd control, and I thanked them as they headed outside.

"Yes," Cash nodded. "Do we have time?"

"Yes," I replied. "You've got at least an hour before lunch."

"Okay," Taylor chimed in, throwing his arm around my shoulders. "Let's do this, but you stay close."

"Alright," I relented, pulling four Sharpie markers out of my back pocket. I didn't even comment on what he said about me staying close. I really hated being looked after. It made me feel incompetent. "It's all yours."

As we pushed the door open, the small crowd cheered for the guys. Ace stopped at the first girl in line, posing for a picture. Braxton opened up and actually smiled for his pictures. The closed off, reserved drummer worked the crowd as if he'd been doing it his entire life.

Taylor scowled at me when I laughed at the group of women who'd surrounded him, lust in their eyes. One girl, no more than twenty years old, stroked his muscular forearm, batting her baby blues at him. I'm sure she'd drop her clothes right there if he'd give the slightest hint of interest.

It took all of twenty minutes for the guys to finish with the fans and climb into the SUV. We headed back to the venue to get ready for another show.

CHAPTER 20

Taylor

Sweat poured down my neck as I sang the chorus to our current single, "As I was". Ace looked over his shoulder and frowned at me. At first, I wasn't sure what the hell he was upset about, but when I followed his line of vision, my heart thundered in my chest.

Doug was in the crowd. I'd know that motherfucker anywhere. The man was tall, like me, but his bulk was not muscular. The man was overweight; his clothes fit tight against his body. He eyed the stage, looking at no one in particular. His blonde hair had grown out since I'd last seen him in Phoenix. Speaking of Phoenix, why the fuck was he here in Nashville?

I backed away from the mic and turned toward the side of the stage, breathing a sigh of relief that Cora was standing there watching us. The song ended and I quickly stepped behind the curtain while Ace talked to the crowd, giving me time to give her a warning.

"What's wrong, Taylor?" she asked, looking confused. I'd never come off the stage before during a show.

"Keep your ass right here," I demanded. "Doug is in the building."

"Fuck," she swore, stepping closer to my side. Thankfully, we'd shown my band the asshole's picture so they could help us keep an eye out for him.

"Call the police," I said. "Do you have your restraining order paperwork with you?"

"Yeah," she scowled. "I swear I'm going to kill that fucker!"

"The hell you will, Coraline," I cursed. "Do what I tell you, and don't you dare leave this fucking spot!" My time was up; I had to get back on stage.

I watched when she grabbed Josh as he made his way up to the side of the stage. She spoke frantically, using her hands to express her frustration. Josh looked over her head and when our eyes connected, he nodded, silently saying he would watch over my girl. Thank God, because it took all I had not to jump off this stage and go beat the fuck out of the man who'd beaten Coraline for walking in on him preparing drugs to sell.

The lights sped up as our song began. It took all of my control keep playing when I lost sight of him. The bastard had turned toward the front doors and slipped outside. It wasn't but a few more minutes before the local police sauntered through the door, their eyes scanning the building for any trouble. Of course, they had no clue who this guy was or what type of damage he'd done to Coraline in Phoenix.

I saw Liam escorting them to the backstage area. Turning toward Coraline, I nodded for her to go on and talk to them. She smiled, but it didn't reach her eyes. We were down to two songs left. Ten more minutes and this concert would be over. I had to make sure she was okay.

As soon as the lights went down, I was off the stage, turning for the door leading to where I knew she was. Kevin was there to take my guitar and to tell me they were in the green room for privacy.

I didn't even knock when I reached the door, pushing it wide open. My eyes landed on Cora, who was sitting on a couch with her arms crossed low over her stomach. As soon as she saw me, her posture changed and she sat up straight…in control. That one action told me that the ever hardened Coraline Maddox was anything other than fine. She was scared, and that realization was like a punch to the gut, because Cora wasn't afraid of anything.

Or so I thought…

"Ms. Maddox," one officer said, standing up with a weary sigh. "We will keep an eye on the building until you are ready to leave town. We've spoken with the detective in Phoenix, and he's determined to get this guy behind bars. My suggestion to you would be to stay with someone while you work, even inside the building. I would like for you to call me when you are leaving the city, just to keep us informed." He handed her a card and shook her hand. The guy didn't offer me any introductions, and that was fine with me. I just wanted to grab Cora and hide her until Doug was caught.

"Hey," she whispered shyly. Her eyes tracked the officers as they left the room. I nodded to the guys, silently telling them we needed some privacy.

"You okay?" I asked, my voice a bit harsher than I'd intended.

"I'm fine," she clipped, gritting her teeth. "I'm just fine, Taylor."

"Cora," I groaned. "What was that?"

"What?" she said, feigning confusion.

"You're scared," I said. It wasn't meant as a question and she damn well knew it. I cupped her face, relaxing when she nuzzled her cheek into my palm. My other hand copied the first, and as I held her tenderly, I saw the fear in her eyes. "He's not going to touch you."

"I hate feeling out of control," she admitted. "I hate having restrictions put on me."

"I know, baby," I whispered, assuring her.

Pulling her to my chest, she didn't complain about my sweaty clothes and let me hold her tightly. This was not the Coraline that everyone knew. This was the woman who let her cousin, and now me, take care of her. She'd fight me tooth and nail, but I was going to have to make her talk to me about what the hell was rolling around in her head concerning the man who'd hurt her. I had a feeling there was something she wasn't telling me.

"I have to work," she blurted, feeling me tense beneath her cheek.

"We need to talk about this," I admonished, tilting her face so that I could capture her lips. The kiss wasn't heated, just a soft press of lips. I nibbled her bottom lip and let her go, pushing her toward the door. "I'm going to shower. I'll find you afterward."

She left with nothing more than a nod, knowing that she couldn't hide anything from me. I was just more attuned to her than she wanted to admit.

CHAPTER 21

Coraline

My hands shook as I hurriedly coiled up
wires and placed them into cases. All of the
guys were working around me while the band
showered and prepared to load up the bus, but
they all had at least one eye on me as I did my
job. I fucking hated it!

I hated that they had to keep checking on me
like some helpless nitwit! I prided myself on the
fact that I didn't need anyone's help in my life.
Yes, my cousin Kane liked to be there when I
needed him, and he helped me though most of
my adolescence, but since he'd begun traveling
with his band, I'd pretty much fended for
myself. When I started working for *Glory Days*
at the age of eighteen, Kane and I were together
constantly. That was why I took my time off on
some private island…to get away from
everyone. Being in L.A. was too damn close to

my father and that was something I tried to avoid like the fucking plague.

Taylor's protectiveness was a different story. There was something about the way he ordered me to listen to him that turned me into an obedient submissive...and I *liked* it. That scared me, too. I shouldn't like being ordered around, because I just wasn't wired that way. I liked my alone time before...but now? I'd give up my free time to spend it in his arms.

I didn't know what the hell it was that made my mind and body respond to his demands, but I wanted it...I craved it. I already knew that I gave up my control when we had sex. Hell, *he* knew that I gave it up to him behind closed doors. I'd never been that way with anyone else in my life. Not that there had been many men keeping my sheets warm, mind you, but Taylor was the only one that I felt I could be myself with at any time. I didn't need to hide behind the bitch mask I so frequently wore.

Taylor didn't let that go to his head. Hell, he seemed to be keeping that little bit of information to himself and not gloating to his buddies that he could order me around when he was buried between my legs. No, he respected that and knew that as soon as my clothes were on, I was back to being my usual tough as nails self. I enjoyed letting him call the shots, but only in private.

Grabbing a rolling cart, I pushed it off to the side of the stage so I could grab another one to start filling up with gear. Liam said he'd take the one I'd just filled out to the trailer and be back to grab another one. Josh and Kevin were finished and said they were going to grab showers. They looked around and noticed several employees still working to clean up the mess left by the patrons at the bar. It looked like they'd be sweeping and wiping down tables for a while longer.

"I'll be okay," I said, gritting my teeth. "There are people around."

After they left, I tried to control my anger at the situation and finish up my job. One of the bartenders turned on some overhead fans and propped open the front door so they could air out the place from all of the cigarette smoke that hung thickly in the air. It wasn't as bad as some of the places I'd been, but it was nice to have someone take the time to clean up the air.

I looked at my phone and frowned when I noticed it'd been about ten minutes since Liam had left with the case. In my daydreaming, I'd lost track of time. He should've been back by now. If he was outside, I could just peek out the back door and yell for him to hurry up.

Grabbing another rolling case, I hurried toward the back door, not seeing any of the guys in the hallway leading to the exit. The lights on the inside of the bus were on, so I figured the band was already inside, preparing for bed.

The black trailer that was pulled behind the bus was open. The door pulled down so that we could roll the cases inside, to be packed accordingly. Just as I rounded the corner, I froze in shock over seeing Liam laying on the ground, his eyes closed as though he'd been sleeping.

"Liam!" I screamed, rushing to his side, but I never made it. Strong hands folded around my throat, squeezing tight and cutting off my breath.

"You fucking bitch!" Doug barked, backhanding me so hard that I fell to my knees. "You cost me a ton of money. It's time you pay up!" He looked haggard, dirty. His jaw had sprouted a patchy, uneven beard. His teeth were yellowed and his dark brown eyes were glassy. He smelled of stale cigarettes and beer.

"Fuck you!" I spat, climbing to my feet. I wouldn't let this guy hurt me again. My lip was swelling, but that would be all he was able to do.

Doug lunged for me, but I sidestepped him and threw a punch to his jaw. He cursed and grabbed my arm, causing me to cry out in pain. "It's time you paid!"

"Yeah, yeah, asshole," I jeered. "You already said that."

"Shut up, bitch," he snarled. Greasy brown hair fell into his eyes as they darkened with lust. I felt a knot at the back of my throat and fear shoot up my spine. He wasn't here just to beat my ass for spilling his precious dope. It was dark out, but the lights outside the building caught on the needle he produced from his pocket. I struggled, pulling at his hold as he uncapped the syringe by putting the cap between his rotten teeth, giving me a creepy smile.

"After you get high, little girl," he mocked, almost demonically. "I'm going to fuck you and you won't even care to fight me." Like most people say…it happened all so fast.

"*Taylor!!!*" I screamed as he plunged the needle in my arm. "What the fuck did you inject me with?"

"Heroin, bitch!" he snarled. I cried out when he tore my shirt, baring my bra covered breasts for his viewing. My body started to sag and my vision blurred.

Oh, God!

My mouth instantly dried, my need for water overpowering almost every other thought. I could've sworn I felt a cool breeze on my legs and warm hands touching my thighs, but I could've been wrong. Why did I feel so warm? Or was it cold? Everything was just so fuzzy.

"*Cora...*"

"*Motherfucker! What did you do to her?*"

"*Police! Call the fucking police!*"

"*Paramedics are coming. Clear her mouth. Check her breathing.*"

Voices…I could hear voices, but I was just too out of it to move. Can I go to sleep now? Please?

"*No, baby. Please. Oh, God…Please, Coraline.*"

So…tired. "Sleep," I mumbled, aloud. Did I say that?

I had no idea what was happening to me or even what was happening in general, but from the frantic voices around me…I knew it wasn't good. The only thing that gave me peace was the scent of fresh rain and manly musk that drifted across my nose.

Taylor was here. He'd take care of me. And this time, I was going to let him do just that, because I was too damn tired to worry about myself.

So, so very tired…

Oh, sweet oblivion…

Sleep…

CHAPTER 22

Taylor

"*Taylor!!!*" I heard Cora scream at the top of her lungs. We all jumped to our feet and ran off the bus. I looked to my right and saw her on the ground and Doug was there, trying to rip her clothes from her body. Anger bubbled to the surface and I felt my heart stop beating.

"NO!" I screamed, racing forward. The bastard dropped something to the ground and looked up as I approached. His eyes flashed fear the moment I tackled him, throwing my fist into his already bloody face.

"Motherfucker! What did you do to her?" I bellowed, twisting his shirt up into my fists, shaking him for an answer.

"Ha!" Doug laughed, but didn't answer me. "I'm paying back your little whore for fucking with me."

"She's not a whore!" I hated that word. I hated that Coraline had used it to describe what she felt like when I didn't call her back. I hate it because she lost our baby…our sweet angel, because she thought I saw her as a whore.

My fists rained down on his face as I heard Ace screaming for someone to call the police and an ambulance. Braxton stopped me from killing the guy by pulling me back as Cash grabbed Doug from his place on the ground.

"I'll kill him!" I raged, trying to push away the hands holding me. My shirt was bunched up around my neck as Braxton kept a tight hold on my upper body by placing a steel arm across my chest.

"Cora needs you," Braxton growled in my ear. "We won't let him get away this time, I promise. She's vomiting, Taylor. I think he shot her up with heroin."

"No!" I choked out, spinning around to see Josh holding her over on her side.

"Don't touch that needle," someone yelled.

Pushing Josh away, I pulled Cora's small body into my arms, stroking her hair away from her face. Her eyes were glassy and unfocused. There was blood on her lip where she'd been hit, the swelling proved that as well.

Sirens wailed off in the distance as I prayed she'd be okay, "Come on, baby. I've got you."

I felt her body convulse again, and I quickly turned her onto her side, but nothing came out when she dry heaved onto the concrete. An officer arrived, squatting down to check over the woman in my arms.

"Can you tell me what she took?" he inquired.

"*She* didn't take anything," I snarled, rage vibrating my voice. "That motherfucker shot her up with what we believe may be heroin. She has a restraining order against him and *he* did this. We need to get her to the hospital."

"What's her name?" he asked.

"Coraline Maddox," I spat out, still watching every rise and fall of her chest.

"This is the lady that two other officers spoke to earlier tonight?" he asked.

"Yes," I replied, sighing in relief as the ambulance arrived. I stood up, ignoring the officer's protest, and walked to meet the paramedics.

"Sir," a paramedic said, stopping me from climbing into the ambulance. "We can take her from here."

"No," I protested, feeling wetness trail down my right cheek. "I'm not leaving her."

"Sir," the other EMT, a woman, interrupted "we have to get an IV started. You can stay with her, but we have to get her to the hospital and she must be looked over. I promise you that she will be in the best hands. You can ride with us."

"Thank you," I slouched, calming only slightly.

Laying her on the stretcher, I took a seat where I was told to and watched as they worked over my girl. She'd never taken drugs a day in her life and that syringe was very large. I hope to hell he didn't overdose her.

"We're ready for transport," the female said, nodding to her partner to close the door.

"Taylor," Cora suddenly croaked, moving her head from side to side. The female paramedic continued hooking her up to monitors and started an IV.

"Right here, baby," I told her, biting my cheek to keep from bursting into tears. She was so tiny, fragile. *God, please don't let this take her from me.*

"Sir?" the paramedic interrupted. "Does she have any allergies we should know about?"

"Not that I'm aware of," I answered, shaking my head. Fuck, I didn't even know anything about her...things that I should know. Hell, when was her birthday? I didn't even know that!

"Was this her first time?" she asked, gently. My eyes shot to the woman, knowing I looked like I was ready to kill someone.

"That guy...he shot her up with something. My drummer said he thought it was heroin. Did you get the needle?" I clasped Cora's hand into mine and stroked the back of her fingers with my thumb. I needed the connection with her. I had to feel her warmth under my hands to prove to myself that she was okay.

"Yes, sir," she nodded. "We will get it analyzed at the hospital."

We arrived at the emergency room and the paramedics rushed Cora inside to be looked at by the doctors. A middle aged nurse pushed me back, saying someone would come talk to me. I had to grab a seat against the wall, because my legs were about to fall out from the stress.

I had to call her cousin. He was going to have to be told and the police in Phoenix would probably want answers.

Kane was also going to fucking kill me for letting her get hurt.

"Hey, man," Kane answered, his voice bright. It was one in the morning in Nashville, but on the West Coast, it was only eleven. Thankfully, I didn't wake him with this news. I needed all of the help I could get to keep him from going ballistic when I told him Coraline's life may be on the line.

"Doug attacked Coraline," I announced, but paused when he let out a string of curses.

"How? What the fuck happened, Taylor?" he demanded.

"I'm not exactly sure, but he got to her and…it's bad, Kane. Really bad," I shuddered, standing up to run my hands through my hair.

"What. The. Fuck. Happened. To. Coraline?" I knew he was going to be pissed, and I knew that he was going to have my ass for this, but I had to tell him.

"The crew was packing up. I left her with Josh and the boys. We all were going to meet on the bus after everything was loaded up and we had all hit the showers. It'd been about an hour when I heard her scream my name. And when I found her, Doug had her on the ground behind the equipment trailer. He…he was tearing off her clothes and he'd injected her with something. We think…we think it may have been a large dose of heroin."

"Oh, my God…No!" he screamed, his voice cracking from the strain. "Where are you? I'm coming."

"Nashville," I said, telling him what hospital we were at and that I wasn't sure how long it would be before I knew anything.

"Was she…," he paused, but I knew what he was asking. Was she raped?

"No," I replied. "I pulled the fucker off of her before he'd ripped all of her clothes off, but that was what he was attempting to do when I found them."

"I hope you killed the motherfucker," Kane roared. I heard a series of doors open and close. He paused in our conversation to relay the information to his wife, Delilah. They had been friends for years, and from what I knew, they were as thick as thieves. I heard Kane's wife crying on the other end of the line, and I swore again that I would kill Doug given the chance.

"Okay," Kane said, after comforting his wife. "I'm bringing the private jet. I'll call you when I have a time of arrival. If anything changes, call me or Ash, okay?"

"Yes," I promised. Looking up, I saw my band rush into the waiting room, behind another stretcher carrying Liam. Josh was stuck to his son's side as they took him back as well. "I'm so sorry, Kane. I failed her."

"You did not fail her," Kane sighed. "I'll be there as soon as I can."

"Thank you," I replied, ending our call.

"Family of Coraline Maddox," a nurse announced. I jumped to my feet and felt Braxton at my back. I wasn't sure if he thought I was going to fall, but I was glad he was there, because the doctor's words were what I'd prayed he would say.

"Is she okay?" I asked, my voice breaking at the end.

"Follow me back to the family room," she motioned, her eyes giving away nothing. "The doctor is waiting for you."

The nurse showed us to a room, not far from the emergency waiting room. She held the door open and nodded to the doctor who was standing in the middle of the small room surrounded by several chairs. A television in the corner was on, showing some infomercial, and the sound was muted.

"My name is Doctor Mason, and I was the doctor who saw Ms. Maddox when she arrived," he paused. "Can you tell me what happened exactly?"

I relayed everything that we knew, even going into detail as to what had happened to her in Phoenix. Doctor Mason took all of the information we gave him and then asked more questions about her general health. It took all of my control not to insist he just get to the point and tell me about Coraline. He finally sighed heavily, running his hand through his light brown hair, and continued.

"The amount of heroin in her system was lethal, but thankfully you got her here in time," Doctor Mason reported. "We've been able to administer an antidote to Ms. Maddox. She is doing much better if you'd like to go in and see her. She's resting now, and we would like to keep her for at least another twenty four hours for observation."

"Is…is she going to be okay?" I asked, praying for good news.

"The medicine we gave her basically cancels out the heroin in her system," he paused again. "With the amount of the drug he gave her, we had to administer it twice. That seems to have done the trick."

"Is she going to have any lasting damage?" I continued asking questions.

"That, we cannot tell right away," he frowned. "She will need to be watched carefully for the next few weeks to months. I was told that she wasn't a drug user, so this could be tricky."

"Tricky?" I growled. "What the hell does that mean?" I felt Braxton lay a heavy hand onto my shoulder, silently telling me to calm the fuck down, but I couldn't.

"She was given an powerful drug…one that millions of people get addicted to every year, Mr. Vaughn. Her body could very well crave this drug now that it's been introduced to her system. She needs to know the signs of that addiction and the people around her need to make sure she doesn't get so bad off that she starts looking for this stuff on the streets. The needle that was used could've been used before, so we've run blood tests on her for a whole host of diseases that she could've been exposed to when she was administered the drug. She will need to be checked periodically by her regular physician to make sure she is healthy."

"That's not going to be a problem. I'll make sure she gets the medical attention she needs and that she is watched for any signs of distress from this," I promised on a growl. "She *will* overcome this."

"That's what I'm praying for," Doctor Mason said, pinching the bridge of his nose. "That woman didn't deserve this, and she could possibly suffer for years to overcome an addiction to something she'd never wanted to try in the first place."

"No she didn't. And I'm glad the asshole responsible is behind bars," I said. "She won't be alone. Coraline has plenty of people to help her." Me, being the one person who would make sure she never suffers from this one day in her life. Kane would give his life to help her too.

"I'll take you back to see her, and once I check on her tomorrow morning, I'll hopefully be able to release her into your care." He told us to follow him to her room as Braxton held the door open.

"I need to call Kane," I mumbled as we followed the doctor out of the waiting room.

"Let's see her first," Braxton said, taking my arm again. "Once you see her, you'll be able to give him a better explanation."

"Okay," I mumbled. I felt as if I were in a fog, not quite believing the things that were happening right in front of my face.

Braxton walked beside me as the doctor lead the way to a bank of elevators. When we arrived on the floor, he stopped at the nurse's station to sign off on what I assumed was an important piece of paperwork in Coraline's chart. He pointed to a door, telling me that was our destination, and I had to take a deep breath when I saw her name written on a board by the room number, 514. The doctor said he'd give us some private time with her and be back to check on her in about an hour, smiling weakly as he returned to the nurse's station.

"I'll wait out here for you," Braxton said, giving my shoulder a squeeze before taking a seat in a chair across the hall from the room.

As I walked toward the bed, I noticed two bags of fluid hanging above her head. A nurse followed me inside and made her way to the sink to wash her hands. Coraline was curled up on her side, facing me, but her eyes were closed as she slept. My eyes bounced all over the room, checking the monitors, hoping they would relay that everything was okay with her. I had no idea what all of those numbers and lines meant on the screens, but I knew the sound of a heartbeat through the monitor, and I sighed heavily when hers was a strong, steady beat.

"We've given her a narcotic antagonist to counteract the drugs she'd been injected with during the incident. Those bags are nothing but saline to keep her hydrated," the nurse spoke softly. "I'll give you a few minutes. My name is Harriet, if you need anything else."

I nodded and waited for the sound of the door closing before I walked up to the bed and sank to my knees.

"Oh, baby," I cried, resting my forehead on her arm. "I'm so sorry."

CHAPTER 23

Coraline

I blinked a few times, squinting against the bright white light that blinded my vision as soon as my eyes cleared enough to tell me I was in a hospital. My body was covered in a white blanket and I burrowed down deeper into its warmth when I felt a cold chill race through my body. My teeth chattered and it took all I had not to break my jaw from the force of trying to keep to tremors at bay.

"Baby?" Taylor whispered. My eyes flashed to my right and there he was...my knight in shining armor, sitting as close to the bed as he could without actually being in it beside me.

"T...Taylor," I shook, looking around the room when I felt my bottom lip start to quiver. When I realized we were alone, I let the first tear fall, but the others afterward did nothing more than pour out of my eyes. I scrambled out of the bed, but Taylor stood quickly and took me into his arms, cradling me against his chest as if I were a small child. I buried my face in his neck as he climbed in the hospital bed, raising it with the remote so that he could sit up with me in his arms.

"Shh, Cora," he cooed, kissing my temple and stroking my short hair. He rearranged the tubes and wires so that I didn't get tangled up in them. "You're okay. You're going to be okay. I've got you...I've got you."

"I'm so c...cold," I complained. Taylor rearranged the blanket around my body that was only covered by a stupid hospital gown. My bare ass sat in his jean covered lap, but I didn't care. He was here and I wasn't dead.

"Lift your feet," he motioned, waiting until I complied to tuck the ends of the blanket under my toes where they rested next to his massive thighs. "Good girl. Let me hold you and get you warm."

"What happened?" I asked, nuzzling my face into neck. His scent washed over me and I felt myself relaxing into his embrace. "I don't remember much."

"Doug injected you with heroin," he growled, tightening his hold when he felt me stiffen. "We were able to get you to the hospital in time to have them give you an antidote to keep you alive. They are going to keep you here for twenty-four hours just to make sure you are okay."

"No," I wimpered. "We have to leave! You'll miss the show in Memphis!"

"It's already been canceled," he informed me, kissing my temple.

"Wait," I froze. "How long have I been here? What day is it?" I was groggy, but not so much that I didn't know what the hell was going on. I knew that I was in a hospital, because the nurse explained everything to me as I was put in this room. She didn't know all of the details, but

I knew Taylor would explain everything to me once he came to my room.

"It's Saturday morning," he answered, closing his eyes. It wasn't until then that I noticed how the skin under his eyes was dark and there was a slight smattering of hair on his face, like he hadn't shaved in a day or two. "You've only been here about eight hours."

"You canceled the show?" I asked, confused. "We can still make it, Taylor."

"No," he said, but there was no demand behind it. It was like he was just too tired to argue with me. "Please, Cora. You are our main priority right now. Plus, the announcement has already been made. We are not doing the show tonight. We will pick back up Tuesday in St. Louis." We had Sunday and Monday off to rest and travel to Missouri. Now, it looked like we would be spending some of that time here in Nashville.

"Am…am I going to be okay?" I had to ask, because the look on his face was honestly scaring me.

"Yes, baby," he nodded. "You are going to be okay, but the doctors are wanting to watch you, and maybe run a few tests on your brain to make sure there was no lasting damage from the heroin."

"How much did he inject me with?" I wondered out loud, not sure if I really wanted to know the answer.

"I don't know the exact dose, but it was enough that it should have killed you," he stopped, trying to compose himself. Taylor stiffened with anger as he talked about what Doug had done. "God, Cora. When I found you…When I saw him *hurting* you, my heart stopped."

"Thank you for saving me," I whispered, placing my cold fingers against the side of his face. Instead of flinching, Taylor closed his eyes again and turned his face to place a kiss to the palm of my hand.

"I'd do it every day for the rest of my life if I had to," he vowed, taking his left hand and cupping my head so he could tuck it into the crook of his neck. "You need to rest. We will talk more once you wake up."

"Okay," I yawned, letting him take over for me, because I was exhausted. As I closed my eyes, letting sleep take me under, I had a feeling that Taylor wasn't telling me everything. It was just that I was too damn exhausted to worry about it at the moment.

My name being called roused me from a deep sleep. I was curled up against a warm muscular body and I couldn't even muster up enough strength to open my damn eyes. I smiled into the cotton shirt that was pressed against my face and let sleep take me once again.

"Coraline, wake up." Taylor's deep voice registered in my brain, but I just didn't want to wake up, unless there was coffee. "Kane's here, baby."

"Kane," I wheezed, my eyes blinking rapidly. Why the fuck was my cousin here at the hospital? Oh, who the hell was I kidding? Kane wouldn't just stay away if I'd been hurt. I'm sure he used the band's private jet to get to my bedside.

"Hey, cuz," Kane smiled, standing next to the bed. He didn't even frown at us when I realized I was still in Taylor's arms. He must've held me while I slept, not moving from the same spot on the bed.

"Hey," I blurted out, biting the inside of my cheek to keep from crying. There were only two men in my life who'd seen me lose control, and both of them were in the room with me. I didn't want to give them any reason to freak the hell out and become even more protective than they already were…especially Kane.

"How are you feeling?" he asked, taking a seat in the chair next to the bed. My eyes danced around the room, checking to make sure we were alone.

"Why are you here?" I questioned, narrowing my eyes. The more I watched my cousin…the more I felt Taylor stiffen against me and I knew I wasn't going to like the answer.

"I'm taking you home," Kane stated. It took a moment for the words to sink in. I knew he was prepared for a fight from me, because he sat forward in his chair and the look of sheer determination flashed across his face. He wasn't going to budge on this.

"No," I snarled. "I'm fine. I'm going to *be* fine!" I pushed myself up and straightened my spine. I would not look weak in front of them, and I sure as hell wasn't going to go back to Los Angeles to lay around doing nothing.

"Just for a week, Coraline," Kane urged, narrowing his eyes before glancing over his shoulder at Taylor.

Why was Taylor not saying anything? Did he not want me here?

"I'm not leaving, Kane," I growled, turning my face so that I was nose to nose with Taylor. "Please don't make me go, Taylor. Please."

"It's for the best, Coraline," he spoke slowly. "You can come back once you are okay, but I can't take care of you on the road. Kane and I want what's best for your health. We don't know what, if any, lasting effects the heroin may have on your system. We want you to see a doctor and make sure you are healthy enough to go back to work. I don't want you doing anything that could cause you to get hurt."

"Did you ever think to ask me what *I* wanted? What *I* thought would be best for *me*?" I snarled. They were ganging up on me and I didn't like it. Backing me into a corner to bully me into doing what they thought was best was not the way to handle things with me. They should know that by now.

Where the hell did they get off making decisions for me? They didn't know what was going on in my mind or my body.

"It's to make sure that you don't become addicted," Kane responded, dropping his hand on my shoulder. "Even if you've never done drugs, your body may begin to crave it, Cora. The doctors want you to be watched for a few days, and I'd feel better if you did that at home."

"That's bullshit," I scoffed. "They gave me an antidote, so it shouldn't be a problem." I tossed my hands in the air in frustration, letting them fall heavy in my lap.

"It's still a dangerous drug that was introduced into your system and no one knows how you will be affected by it," Taylor added. "Please, Coraline. I can't take care of you and still do my job..."

"You know what?" I shouted, cutting him off. I scrambled out of Taylor's lap, slapping his hand away when he reached out to steady me as I wobbled on my bare feet. "Fuck you, Taylor Vaughn. I don't need a fucking babysitter, and I sure as fuck do not need you to choose between me and your job! GET OUT!"

"Cora," he warned, his green eyes going dark, darker than I've ever seen them. I had to look away from both of the men in my life that wanted to shield me from everything. I wasn't a child, but they were sure as hell acting like I was.

"Get. OUT!" I wrapped the blanket around my body and climbed back into the hospital bed, anger boiling in my veins. When Taylor started walking toward me, I pointed my finger toward the door again and said, "Get the fuck out of here! Both of you!"

The two men froze for only a moment, but it didn't take them long to realize I wasn't kidding. I flinched when they both leaned over and kissed my forehead before silently leaving me alone. I couldn't believe they had just *decided* what I was going to do. No one...and I mean *no one* would tell me how to deal with shit in my life. No...not anymore.

It wasn't their place to make those decisions for me. I was a grown ass woman and didn't need their permission to get more medical help. The antidote canceled out the drugs that Doug injected into my body. I didn't crave that high or whatever the hell you called that episode that happened. The last thing my body wanted to do was relive that horrible event.

And if they thought for one damn minute that I would go quietly back to Los Angeles like a good little girl and sit on my ass when I could be working, they obviously are not as smart as I gave them credit for. Oh, hell to the no! I'll just pack my bags and find a deserted island somewhere in the Caribbean to spend the rest of the time off from work. I didn't need Taylor

Vaughn to keep an eye on me so he could do his job. I didn't need him.

If I didn't need him, then why the hell was I frantically wiping the steady stream of tears that were falling from my eyes?

CHAPTER 24

Taylor

"Well, that didn't go very well," Kane snickered, trying to keep a straight face.

"No," I tucked my chin, fighting the urge to grin. "I'd say that didn't go very well at all."

"Stubborn ass woman," Kane lamented. When our eyes connected, I saw the corners of his crinkle, and we both burst out laughing for all we were worth. "She's not going to come home with me. You know this, right?"

"Yeah," I concurred, shaking my head slightly. "She's going to do what she wants to do."

We'd stepped out of Coraline's room and found a set of chairs a few doors down to sit. I took the seat that gave me a direct line of sight to her room. Even I could admit that I had a feeling she would bolt. She'd run and never come back to me if she felt like she was being cornered. That's exactly what we'd done, too.

"When is the doctor expected to come back?" Kane asked. He leaned forward, resting his elbows on the tops of his legs, sighing heavily when he ran his hands through his hair.

"Around noon," I told him. "He may release her this afternoon, but I'm not certain."

"So, where do you go from here?" he asked.

"I march right back in that room and take her with me to Kansas City," I vowed, taking a deep breath and standing to my full height. I was tired of this fucking game of chase Cora and I had been caught in over the past few months. She was mine and it was time I claimed her. "She's mine, Kane. Your cousin owns my fucking heart, and I'm not going to let her run from me again."

"You love her?" he stammered, clearing his throat. When I looked up into his eyes, I could see how much he and Cora looked alike. The fire she had in her hazel gaze was staring back at me from the man standing in front of me, staking his big brother rights on protecting her.

"I do love her," I beamed. "She loves me, but she hasn't admitted it. I promise you, I will make her happy, but I'm not going to ask for your blessing."

"No," he laughed. "No, I don't think my blessing will amount to a hill of beans, because it's Coraline Maddox's blessing you are looking for when it comes to this."

"You know what?" I grinned, looking over at the door to her room. I didn't even wait for his reply to finish what I was going to say. "You are absolutely right."

"Yes, I am," he snorted, slapping my shoulder in a way that told me he was happy for us. "I'm going to go grab something to eat. I'll be back shortly."

"Okay," I said, turning in the direction to go claim my girl. "I'm not going anywhere."

"Make her happy, Taylor," he warned.

"You have nothing to worry about there, Kane," I promised, throwing out a goodbye over my shoulder. I didn't really pay much attention to her cousin as I grabbed the handle, shoving it wide open and causing the door to hit the wall behind it with too much force.

"Jesus Christ, Taylor," she clutched her chest. "Are you trying to give me a heart attack?"

When she looked up, all of the color drained from her face, seeing me standing in the doorway with my arms crossed across my chest. I knew I looked menacing just standing there, but I was tired of this bullshit we'd been going through for what seemed like forever. If I really looked back, it'd been almost two years since I'd met the little firecracker that was Coraline Maddox. And I swear I'd known, even then, that she was going to be mine.

"What the hell is wrong with you?" She sat up in the bed and I noticed that she'd changed into her street clothes and had the small backpack I'd brought her sitting on the chair next to her bed.

"Going somewhere?" I gritted the question through my teeth and used my chin to jut out toward the bag.

"Uh...yeah," she responded, clearing her throat a few times because she was nervous.

"Where?" I demanded, knowing damn good and well, either she was going to tell me or lie her way out of this room and go to an airport so she could run.

"I'm supposed to be released this afternoon," she mumbled, her voice small and wavering. "So, I'm just getting ready to go. I hate hospitals."

"Liar," I growled, dropping my arms and taking one step toward her. She froze, her eyes widening with some form of fear. I didn't like that look at all, so I relaxed my jaw so that I didn't look like a deranged killer.

"That's just plain mean, Taylor," she complained, placing a hand on her hip. As I approached, I noticed that the dark circles under her eyes had lighted substantially since she arrived at the hospital. Her bottom lip was still swollen, but nowhere near as bad as it was when we arrived.

"You're running away from me, aren't you?" I fumed, coming to a stop right next to the bed. Bending at the waist, I pressed my forehead to hers and closed my eyes for just a moment, inhaling her delicious scent.

"Yes," she admitted, causing my eyes to open wide. Her nose crinkled and she rubbed her forehead against mine. "I was going to run away."

"Not happening, baby," I announced. "The only place you are going is with me…nowhere else. Got it?"

"But…Kane," she halted, her eyes searching mine for something. I didn't know what it was that she needed to see in my eyes, but I'd let her look all fucking day if that's what she needed to assure herself.

"Kane went to get something to eat and to give us some privacy," I said. "He'll be back in a little while."

"Okay," she sighed, relaxing and leaning back in the bed. The upper half was raised, so she ended up in a sitting position with a few pillows behind her head. I nudged her hips with my hand until she scooted over enough for me to take a seat next to her.

"Coraline," I started, taking her tiny hand into mine. When she looked up at me, I pulled her into a fierce hug, burying my face into her neck, the only place I'd ever found comfort. Pressing a tender kiss to the skin there, I pulled back slightly and bumped our foreheads together.

"Taylor?" she questioned, her beautiful hazel eyes drowned with worry.

"I love you," I said. "I think I've always loved you, Coraline. I'm tired of you running...hell, I'm begging you not to run from me, because I need you. You are my lifeline, baby."

"You love me?" she gasped.

"Yeah," I said, stroking her cheek with my thumb. "I do."

"I've loved you since you tied me to your bed on that island," she admitted. "I wanted to hate you, but I just...couldn't." She wrapped both arms around my neck, tugging me forward.

"I'm sorry for not calling you back," I said, repeating the words I'd already told her a million times over. "I'll never forgive myself for not being there for you. I'll never fail you again, Cora."

"You didn't fail me, Taylor," she stared into my eyes, shaking her head slightly. "I don't think we can put a label on whose situation was worse than the others. I think that we both had been dealt a shit card and we had to grow from those experiences alone so that we could be stronger together. Can we start over? I mean, really start over again?"

"Yeah, baby," I smiled at her, seeing light come back to my girl's eyes. "You're mine now, Coraline Maddox, and it's my job to take care of you, starting with this situation."

I looked into her eyes, the ones that were light with happiness, suddenly darkened with anger. "I'm not leaving."

"Coraline," I begged.

"No," she glowered, taking my hand and squeezing it tight. "I've never run from my problems, and going back home right now is not what I want or need to do. I need to work. I need to be with you. Please...*please* don't send me away. If anything, I need your strength through this. If I end up getting an addiction from this, you are the only one I want beside me. *You* won't let this take me. I know you won't."

With every word, tears gathered in her eyes until they were nothing but heavy pools of liquid that could no longer hold their banks. My hands cupped her face as the tears spilled over, catching on my thumbs. My lips pressed to hers soundly, not moving back until I couldn't hold my breath any longer.

"Oh, God, baby," I panted. "I'll not let this hurt you. I promise." This was a vow I would make with blood if that was what it took to keep the promise of making sure she was okay.

"I know you won't," she told me, a soft lift to the corner of her plump lips.

"So, you're not coming home with me," Kane announced from the door. We both gasped and turned to see her cousin, the only man in her life besides myself that cared for her deeply, standing there with one hand on the door, and the other on his hip.

"No," she blushed. "No, Kane. I'm staying with Taylor."

"You'll call?" he grilled, moving from the door to the side of the bed.

"Yes," she sighed, rolling her eyes. "I'll call you."

"Okay," he laughed. "It's about damn time." With that, Kane Maddox turned around and left the room, but not before looking over his shoulder, motioning for me to follow.

"I'll be right back," I smirked.

"He better not try to kick your ass," she fussed.

Standing up, I cupped her chin again and placed a sweet kiss to her lips, pulling away before I decided to push things further. As it was, I had to adjust myself to keep from walking out to talk to her cousin with a raging hard on.

"He won't," I promised, making my way to the door.

Of course, my promise was short lived when the front of my shirt was bunched up into a large fist with the word "FREE" tattooed across the knuckles and I was pushed against the wall. Half a second later, Kane Maddox was in my face, his eyes were so dark, they were almost black.

"I swear to God if you fucking hurt her again," he breathed, anger fueling his words. I didn't stop him, because I got it...I understood where he was coming from and if I were in his place, I'd be doing the same damn thing. "I *will* kill you."

"I wouldn't stop you," I let him know, tilting my head to the side. "Are you going to punch me or can I get back to my girl so I can take her home to meet my family?"

"Yeah, man," Kane said, letting go of my shirt, but not before giving me a hard shove. "Keep my cousin safe."

I gave him a few minutes to say his goodbyes to Coraline. After a tight bro hug, he departed and I returned to the room. She was laying on her side. Her beautiful smile almost brought me to my knees. There was so much love and trust in them that my steps faltered.

Knowing that I was going to be responsible for another human being's welfare and happiness should have scared me senseless, but it didn't. The thought of not having this little pixie in my life was an even worse nightmare.

"Are you ready to go back to work, baby?" I teased, taking a seat on the edge of her bed. When I opened my arms in a silent demand for her to come to me, she leapt into my lap and let me nuzzle my face into her sweet smelling neck.

Home. Coraline Maddox was my home.

CHAPTER 25

Coraline

"My parents are going to love you," Taylor stated.

We were currently in the back of a rented Tahoe, being driven to Taylor's parents' house outside of Kansas City, MO. Looking out the window, I smiled at the sunny day that greeted us as we traveled.

I leaned my head over on Taylor's shoulder and inhaled his masculine scent. For some reason, that scent calmed me, and as nervous as I was at the moment, it was something I was a very grateful for. I rubbed my hand up his muscular arm, feeling the warmth under my fingertips. He wore a pair of black denim jeans that hugged his thick thighs and a pair of boots that fell open at the tops. His shirt was an old, white *Glory Days* tee from a few years ago. He'd already torn the sleeves off, and the neckline was a tattered mess, but it looked amazing on him.

"I'm hoping so," I chuckled nervously. I didn't date much because of my line of work, and meeting a guy's parents wasn't something I was used to doing. Hell, now that I look back, I don't think I'd ever met any parents of the guys I dated.

"What has you smiling?" he asked, taking his thumb and stroking my bottom lip.

"Just thinking," I blushed. I thought maybe I could get away with my vague answer, but when he raised his brow for me to continue, I couldn't deny him. "I've never met the parents of a guy I've been with or dated...ever."

"Good," he looked pleased. The quirk in his lip was possessive, and I shook my head at that because Taylor had claimed me as his in the hospital, and I found that I liked knowing that more than I should. I used to roll my eyes at my cousin and all of his alpha growling ways with his wife, but now I understood the dreamy look she'd get in her eyes when he would claim her as his. Now, I'm probably doing the same damn thing when Taylor goes around growling *mine* at every man who walks within ten feet of where I'm standing.

After Kane and Taylor had their pissing match over me and my well-being, I was discharged and told to see a doctor if I had any strange side effects from the heroin that'd been injected into my body by Doug. So far, I have had no lasting problems, but then again, it'd only been three days.

As we pulled into a long dirt driveway, I noticed that the scenery didn't match the man sitting next to me. Outside my window, there was a field with about fifty black cows lazily munching on blades of grass, a few little calves hanging close to their mommas.

"You're a farm boy?" I giggled.

"I never fit in here," he muttered, but it wasn't a sad admission. "I just wanted to play the guitar and travel. My parents used to tease me about spreading my wings and flying away as soon as the candles were blown out on my eighteenth birthday cake. They weren't too far off." He squeezed my hand as we pull to a stop, but I didn't have time to say anything before an older couple rushed out the door, making quick work of getting to the vehicle.

"Oh, son!" his mom squealed. "Look at you!"

"Hey mom," he replied, a slight blush creeping up his cheeks.

"Son," his father grinned, taking him into a huge bear hug.

Looking at his mother, I could see where he got his stunning green eyes. Although hers were weathered, they still held the spark true to Taylor's own emerald gaze. His father was just as tall and bulky as his son, but his skin was darkened naturally from years of working outside.

"Is this Coraline?" his mom asked, holding out a hand for me to shake. I stepped forward slightly, but when our fingers touched, I was pulled into an unexpected hug. "She's beautiful, Taylor!"

"Mom," he grunted, pulling me away from his mother's cuddling. I really didn't mind it. In fact, I liked it a lot. The feel of a mother's hug, no matter if that woman gave birth to you or not, was one of the best feelings in the world.

"It's nice to meet you," his father announced, taking my hand into a firm handshake.

"Thank you Mr. and Mrs. Vaughn, for having me over," I responded, using the politeness I'd learned from hanging at Kane's house when we were kids.

"Please, dear," his mom chuckled. "Call me Mary, and Taylor's father, George. Come in…Come in! We only have a few hours!"

"Calm down, mom," Taylor laughed, again. "We have time."

Inside the house, I felt a sense of calm wash over me. The front room was as cozy as something you'd see in a magazine. An old barn door was the focal point on the large wall to my right. It looked as if it'd come straight from outside and was hung with pride in the family's living room. The wood was old and cracked, but weathered beautifully. Taylor took my hand and pulled me into the kitchen where a large rectangle table sat. The dark wood matched the wall hanging in the other room and had enough chairs for ten people.

"Would you like a glass of tea?" Mary asked.

"Please," I replied. "May I help you with anything?"

"Oh, no," she smiled, sliding a glass over to my awaiting hands. "Grab a seat, dear. Tell me all about this tour."

We spent the better part of an hour talking about where we'd been and about the new album. Taylor's parents were extremely proud of him, and I found myself falling in love with his family. As I sat back and looked around the room, seeing pictures of Taylor when he was younger, I realized I kept swallowing a knot of hope in my throat. I didn't want to lose my shit and cry in front of his folks, but damn, I forgot how it felt to have a *real* family. Mine had been broken for so long.

"Come take a walk with me," Taylor conspired, causing me to jump. I didn't realize he had moved and was now sitting so close I could feel his warm breath on my neck. When I blinked, I felt my cheeks blush when I noticed his parents had left the table and were busy making lunch in the kitchen.

"I'm sorry," I whispered. "Lost in my thoughts."

"I know," he said, simply.

Taylor grasped my hand and pulled me along behind him as he made his way out of the back door. The back porch stretched the length of the house and I laughed when he jumped off, landing at the bottom of the steps. He reached out and tugged my hand, causing me to squeal when he hauled me up so I was on his back.

"We are going to the barn," he proclaimed, tightening his arms under my knees. I kissed the top of his head and wrapped my arms around his neck, but not hard enough to choke him.

As we reached the barn, I noticed several horses standing in a fenced in area off to the left of the building. "They are so pretty," I said, eyeing the majestic animals standing there watching as we move past them.

"One of them is mine," he pointed out, jutting his chin in their general direction. "The black one. Her name is Mercy."

"I've never ridden a horse," I shared, not even knowing why I said that.

"Well, maybe we can come back to visit and I'll teach you," he decided, loosening his hold on my legs and letting me slide down his back as we reached the barn doors. I let him pull it open, leaving just enough room for us to walk inside.

The interior of the barn was something straight out of a western movie. There were six stalls to my right, all with name placards for the horses. There were several ribbons on the wall to my left, showing that the horses were winners of some show the year before. On the left side of the barn, several bales of hay were stacked next to blue drums that I assumed held feed.

My assessment of the barn was cut short when Taylor spun me around so that I fell softly against his chest. He didn't speak words when he cupped my face with both hands, swooping in to press his lips to mine.

He'd kissed me many times before, but there was something different about the way he possessed my lips this time. His desperation poured from every caress and nibble to my bottom lip. He silently urged my mouth to part with a heated swipe of his tongue. I panted heavily when his need for me increased. I felt the wetness pool between my legs and I found myself shamelessly rubbing my sex against his muscular thigh.

"I fucking love you, Coraline Maddox," he panted. He continued to pepper my cheek, jaw, and neck with hot, wet kisses. If I didn't know any better, I'd think he was trying to memorize my taste.

"I love you too, Taylor," I moaned. His hands had moved from my face to my neck, and then around to my ass, squeezing the globes with enough pressure to get his point across. "We can't do this in the barn!"

"Shush," he muttered, lifting me up into his arms. My legs automatically wrapped around his waist and I found myself grinding my pussy against his stomach. "Fuck, baby."

"Taylor," I purred, cupping his face and bringing his lips back to mine. Damn, I knew we wouldn't be doing it in the barn, but when he wrapped his strength around me, I felt my body weep for him.

He started moving, walking briskly to the set of stairs I had noticed earlier. I started to protest, but he silenced me with a swat to my ass and another growl. Opening my eyes, I noticed the loft was covered with more bales of hay, some of them were stair stepped in height.

As soon as my ass hit the spot he'd moved us to, Taylor grabbed the hem of my blue t-shirt and hefted it up over my head, his face landing between my breasts. The cups of my black lace bra were tucked under each breast immediately. I threw my head back and let out a curse when he took one of my nipples between his teeth, biting down with just the right amount of pressure. As he worshipped them, I pulled on his shirt until he released my nipple with a pop so that he could discard his own clothing.

My hands fumbled with his belt and the button fly of his jeans. As soon as his fly was opened, I found my hand cupping his heavy erection, my fingers dancing along his velvety length. I rubbed my thumb across the top, gathering the little bead of moisture at the tip. I heard his groan of approval, but he never did release my breasts that were now being roughly cupped with his massive hands.

"Please, Taylor," I begged, reaching for the button to my own jeans.

"Mine," he grunted, pushing my hands away so that he could divest me of the only remaining barrier between our heated bodies.

My tennis shoes were tossed to the side and my pants were off, laying inside out somewhere on a hay bale to my right. I squeaked when a piece of hay poked me in the ass, slapping Taylor on the arm when he just chuckled.

My look of outrage at his laughter died quickly when he dropped to his knees and buried his face between my legs, nibbling on my sex. His hands gripped tightly to my inner thighs, pushing them out to the side so that he could fit his broad shoulders comfortably. Two fingers entered me swiftly, rubbing that spot that drove me crazy. He knew when he found that trigger, because his moan against the lips of my sex was that of a man pleased with what he was doing.

"Give it to me, Coraline," he demanded. "Come for me, baby."

"Oh, God," I gasped, feeling my body hum. The second he bit down on my clit, I was flying. "More...Oh...Taylor...Fuck!"

Before I could come down from the amazing release he had given me, Taylor lined up and pushed forward, seating himself balls deep inside me. His arm looped around my back, and his warm chest pressed against my own. My nipples rubbed deliciously against his chest when he started to pound into my body, soft grunts echoing off the walls of the barn.

God, it felt amazing being in his arms. This raw, unexpected coupling just tightened the connection between us. I felt him not only in my arms, but in every pore of my body. He was here, with me...holding me...loving me to completion.

"One more, Cora," he demanded, tangling his fingers in the back of my head, forcing our mouths together. His tongue mimicked what his cock was doing, showing me exactly what I'd missed from the island. "Let go, baby. Let go for me."

His words were what I needed. The spoken command to give him my control. To let him be in charge of my pleasure was one of the hardest things I'd imagined letting happen, but it was easier than I'd previously thought. He would take the reins of my desire and grasp them securely in his strong hands, never letting anyone or anything else be in control. As long as Taylor was by my side, I knew he would be the one to take care of me, but only when I needed taking care of.

"Taylor...with me...please," I panted, each word forced out with each of his thrusts.

"I'm so there, baby," he said, burying his face in my neck. "I love you, Coraline."

"And I love you, Taylor," I breathed. "Now, make me come."

He didn't need to be told twice. Taylor slid the hand that was cupping my head down my side and wedged it between our bodies. The moment he pressed his thumb to my clit, I lost all sense of reasoning. We both cursed out loud as our climaxes reached their peak.

His head moved so that he could press his forehead to my own. Our breathing didn't want to slow and I laughed when I felt his cock jump inside me, hardening quickly. "We can't do that again. You parents may come looking for us."

"We don't want that," he joked, his eyes widening at my words.

I let him help me dress, and after we picked out several pieces of straw from our hair, we made our way back inside, where we were met with lunch. It took us another hour before we were finally able to say goodbye with a promise to return at Christmas, just after the end of their tour. We held hands on the way back to the arena, but I was lost in thought.

How the hell was I going to be able to work a relationship with Taylor Vaughn, when I refused to leave my cousin in the dark? I had some thinking to do, but things would work out, because I wouldn't let anymore heartache befall

me. We'd both had enough of that between the

two of us to last a lifetime.

CHAPTER 26

Taylor

It was nearing three o'clock in the afternoon when we arrived at the venue. Braxton was sitting in a lawn chair by the bus, a baseball cap pulled low over his eyes. I assumed he was asleep, but once he heard the Tahoe come to a stop, he pushed the bill of his cap up and out of the way, greeting us with a small smile.

"How are the parents?" he asked.

"Same as always," I shrugged, but the shit eating grin didn't leave my face as I watch Cora head through the back door of the venue. She'd already bitched me out for having her back late, and the guys were going to give her hell for not being there on time. I just told her that I was the boss, and they could just get over it. That got me an eye roll that had me kissing the sass right out of her in the backseat.

"You look like a lovesick fool," Ace teased, stepping off the bus.

"That's because I am," I admitted, proudly. "She's finally mine, and I'm not letting her go."

"I hate to be the one to address the big, fucking elephant in the room," Cash said, narrowing his eyes at me. "But how the hell are you going to steal her away from Kane?"

"That, I don't know," I admitted.

"Well, you need to figure that shit out," he replied, slapping my back as he walked past to go inside.

"He's right," Braxton agreed.

"I'll talk to her," I said, hoping they'd just shut up and let me have a moment where I could just enjoy the fact that Cora was mine and there were no issues with her health at present.

A hissing sound caused us to look up toward the gate. A sleek, black tour bus rounded the corner, announcing that our opening band, *Witch's Spawn*, was arriving right on schedule.

Ace tossed his empty water bottle in the trash and walked with purpose toward the bus as it came to a stop just on the other side of ours.

It seemed that Grant "Ace" Ryker had been a little overly helpful with the lead singer of *Witch's Spawn*, Pressley Pittman. The last few shows, I noticed how he would go out of his way to talk to her, even going so far as to sit out by the soundboards during their show. His eyes never left the stage, even when several female fans would basically throw themselves at him as he made his way through the crowd.

Sure as shit, Presley rounded the front of the buses and Ace was there, showing his charm and smiling like a fucking dog in heat. The sexy lead singer just smiled and answered whatever he was asking, taking a moment to wave to Braxton and me as we stood watching our fearless leader slobber all over her. As soon as they were in the building, Braxton and I laughed until we both had tears in our eyes.

"He's next," Braxton chuckled, jutting his chin out toward our singer. "First you, and now him. I'm never letting a woman lead me around by my balls."

"Oh, but it's so satisfying when they do," I teased, bumping shoulders with the man who never cracked a joke. It was nice to see this side of him. He was always very brooding and stoic, never dropping his hard ass features.

"Go find some work," he griped, settling back into his usually grumpy self. "I'll meet you inside."

It didn't take long before Coraline took a break for dinner. The venue catered our food for the night. They had their own cook and he served whatever the hell he wanted, but we were not complaining. Hamburgers and hotdogs were always welcomed when they didn't come from a fast food joint.

I'd just made myself and Cora a plate when she drug herself over to the couch, looking exhausted. "Thank you," she mumbled, accepting the plate I handed her. She made quick work of her meal, before laying on her side and resting her head in my lap. It was only six o'clock, and we had an hour before doors opened, so I let her sleep, but I wanted her comfortable. She'd only been out of the hospital three days. And as much as I wanted to demand she stay on the bus, I knew that she would kick my ass for suggesting such a thing.

I made my excuses and picked up my girl, carrying her out to the bus. When I reached our bunk, I carefully laid her down and whispered for her to scoot over. I pulled off her tennis shoes and made quick work of my own. I climbed inside and closed my eyes, happy that I could get some rest before the show.

Tiny fingers danced across my chest and immediately flicked my nipple piercing, causing my cock to harden painfully in my jeans. "If you keep doing that, we will never go inside."

"Hmm," she moaned, pressing a kiss to the cross tattoo on my side.

"I love you," I whispered, pulling her closer. "I want to talk to you about something."

"Anything," she mumbled, her eyes blinking away the sleep.

"I want you to stay on with us," I said, dropping the bomb that we all were worried about happening. "I know you are Kane's, but baby, I don't know if I can let you go away from me for that long."

"I know," she exhaled, reaching up to run her fingers over my jaw. "And I've been thinking."

"Yeah?" I asked, hopeful.

"I think, for now, I'd like to do both," she paused, pressing a finger to my lips when I started to protest. "Just for a little while, Taylor. Rita is ready to take over for me. I think I can get her trained during the first leg of their next tour. After that, I will be yours. I'll work with you and when we are free, we could maybe go to a resort and spend some time…alone."

"I'd like that very much," I replied, smiling like a damned fool, but I didn't care. The pressure of worry eased off my chest and damn, it felt good knowing that she'd be mine.

"I have another request," I said, worried how my next question would go over. We hadn't talked about the baby. Well, not in detail, and I knew it bothered her that she didn't know what the baby's sex would've been. It bothered me, too. I needed closure.

"What?" she asked, propping herself up on an elbow. I rolled to my side and mimicked her pose, so that we were eye to eye.

"I would like to get a new tattoo," I paused, inhaling deep. "I'd like to get a small pair of angel wings on my wrist with "Angel" underneath them…for the baby. I know that we will never know if it was a boy or a girl, but I'd at least like to give it a name. I think Angel would be perfect."

I felt her body shake, seconds before I heard the heart-shattering sob that wrenched from her chest. My arms immediately wrapped around her, pulling her as close to my chest as I could without hiding her under my skin.

"I'm sorry. Maybe I shouldn't have said anything," I said, rocking Cora in my arms and letting her cry against my chest.

"No…no," she said, shaking her head. "I love it, Taylor. I never thought you'd want to name the baby."

Hooking a finger under her chin, I pulled her to where I could look into her hazel eyes. Seeing the tears in them killed me, absolutely gutted me.

"Don't cry, baby," I begged. "I want to do it after the show tonight. I have a place that's only a few blocks from here and I know the guy."

"I want one, too," she admitted. "Can I get the same one?"

"Matching, yeah?" I asked, hopeful.

"Yeah," she smiled.

"I think that would be amazing," I said, pressing my lips to hers. They tasted of her tears and love. I couldn't even tell you how long we stayed in our embrace before Ace came out to the bus, cursing for all he was worth. We were late, and it was time to get back to work.

"After the show?" I asked as we walked hand in hand through the doors.

"Yes," she smiled, standing on the tips of her toes to kiss my cheek. "Go, play your heart out and let's get started on our life together."

"On it, boss," I laughed, smacking her ass as I made my way up on the stage. Looking over my shoulder, I tossed a wink at her and found my mark on stage. The lights came up and I smiled the entire night, knowing that the little pixie was mine.

As we emerged from the tattoo parlor, I flipped over our joined hands and stared at the tiny reminder of our combined love. The tattoo wasn't much, but it was enough to remember our Angel.

"I love you, Coraline Maddox," I said, taking her face gently in my hands. "It's time for us to move forward. No more running, right?"

"No, Taylor," she agreed, shaking her head and looking at the matching angel wings on our wrists. "No more running. I love you."

"I knew you would," I chuckled, picking her up and spinning her around on the sidewalk outside of the tattoo parlor.

I kissed her in front of the world to see, because I'd finally found my place in the world, next to the stubborn little roadie who owned my heart.

EPILOGUE

Taylor

Four months later…

A week. That's all we had to get my shit packed up into boxes and moved to Los Angeles before we were due back on the road. I'd put my place up for sale a month and a half ago after confiding in Cora that I needed to get away from Seattle and start over. When she told me that she wanted to stay in L.A. so she could be close to her cousin, I told her that I would start looking for a place near her condo. She laughed at me and told me that I didn't need to do that because we already had a place, and she had plenty of room to store all of my equipment. So, in not so many words, Coraline Maddox asked me to move in with her and I happily agreed.

"Where the hell is Kane?" she growled, almost losing her balance reaching for some cups on the top shelf of my kitchen cabinet. I rushed up behind her, placing my hands on her hips to steady her. The little pixie couldn't reach the shelf from the ground, so she climbed up on the counter and stood there like she owned the place.

"He said he'd be here in an hour," I responded, sliding my hands from her hips upwards, slipping them under her shirt. Her soft skin met my fingertips and I looked up to see her beautiful hazel eyes darkening as she watched my hands move around to her stomach.

"Oh, really?" she smirked. I felt her body shiver and I knew it had nothing to do with the cold.

"Come here," I barked, a little harsher than I'd intended.

My lips crashed down on hers, nibbling and demanding entrance. When I felt her tiny tongue press against mine, I was lost. We'd only been home twenty four hours and there had been hardly any packing done since we'd quickly realized we didn't have to sneak out to the bus for a fast romp in the bunks. My bedroom furniture was already broken down, the mattresses lying flat on the ground, but that didn't stop us. Hell, I'd taken her against the wall three times already.

"We need to hurry," she breathed against my neck.

Wrapping an arm around her waist, I lifted her off of her feet and made quick work of her jeans, pulling them off in one fell swoop. I did nothing more than yank my fly down before entering her swiftly. I carried her to the kitchen table, which we'd found was the perfect height, and thrust deep several times. Soft mewls escaped her lips when I pushed her shirt and bra up around her neck. When she lifted her hands above her head, I paused in removing her shirt right to the point that it covered her eyes. My left hand grasped her tiny wrists, pinning them to the table.

"Feel, Cora," I hissed, biting her earlobe and finding pleasure when she let out a soft gasp. "Let me love you."

"Please?" she begged.

My lips found a rosy nipple, biting and sucking on it until it peaked tightly against my tongue. Repeating the process with the other one, I felt her clamp down on my cock and I knew she was close.

"Come for me, Cora," I demanded. "Come on, baby."

"Help me, Taylor," she said, thrashing her head from side to side. "I...I can't."

"You better come before your cousin gets here," I warned. I smiled to myself when I heard her gasp. The idea that we could get caught caused her to pause. I pumped faster, urging her to let go. When she kept moving her head from side to side, I used my other hand to reach between our bodies and circle her clit, pressing hard when I felt her go liquid around my cock.

"That's it," I said. "Come for me, Coraline."

"Yesss," she screamed, her release striking just as a fissure of awareness crawled up my spine. I felt myself let go and I collapsed when my body was finally spent.

We hurried to get cleaned up and thankfully we did, because her cousin showed up earlier than he'd said. I finger combed my hair and walked to the door, laughing when he walked in and looked at the place.

"What the hell have you two been doing? You should've packed more than this by now," he cursed, glaring daggers at me. I could only laugh. "Oh, God! I really don't want to fucking know."

"Let's get to work," I chuckled. "Thanks for coming over."

"Yeah, well," he scoffed. "Once you move to Los Angeles, I'm going to have to remember to call you ahead of time, and not just show up at Cora's place unannounced."

"Yeah," I said, slapping him on the back. "That might be a good idea."

We worked for the better part of three days, throwing out things I wouldn't need and packing the things I did. The last night in my old house was not a sad night for me. It was a beginning…a beginning with the little pixie roadie who'd stolen my heart and gave me something to live for.

The End…

About Theresa Hissong:

Theresa is a mother of two and the wife of a retired Air Force Master Sergeant. After seventeen years traveling the country, moving from base to base, the family has settled their roots back in Theresa's home town of Olive Branch, MS, where she enjoys her time with family and old friends.

After almost three years of managing a retail bookstore, Theresa has gone behind the scenes to write romantic stories with flare. She enjoys spending her afternoons daydreaming of the perfect love affair and takes those ideas to paper.

Look for other exciting reads...coming very soon!